"Take me away," Shanal implored.

It was the last thing Raif expected the bride to say in the middle of her wedding ceremony.

"Take me far away, right now."

"Are you sure?" he asked.

"Just, *please*, get me out of here," she begged, her bewitching pale green eyes shining with unshed tears.

It was the tears that undid him. A taxi rounded the corner. Raif secured Shanal's small hand in his and pulled the runaway bride to her feet.

"C'mon," he said, as he bolted for the sidewalk, towing Shanal along behind him.

He raised his hand to get the cabbie's attention. Eyes round as saucers and his mouth hanging open, the cabbie stopped and Raif yanked open the back door and guided Shanal inside.

Shanal sat next to him, pale but finally more composed, as they pulled away from the curb and down the street.

Raif cast one look through the back window. The crowd on the sidewalk outside the cathedral had grown.

In its midst stood the groom, his eyes fixed on the retreating cab. Even from this distance Raif felt a prickle of unease. Burton, understandably, did not look happy.

But Raif was getting exactly what he wanted.

* * *

The Wedding Bargain is part of The Master Vintners series: Tangled vines, tangled lives.

* * *

If you're on Twitter,
tell us what you think of Harlequin Desire!
#harlequindesire

Dear Reader,

When I first embarked upon The Master Vintners series I had only the first two books clear in my head, and now we're up to book six, the last of the series.

Writing a series is always fun for me and this is the longest one I've done to date. There's always plenty to keep track of and I have a notebook filled with tables and character descriptions and pictures of everyone, and I've tried to keep all the threads from becoming too entangled. When I visited Adelaide a few years ago, I found the area to be incredibly inspiring. It is a beautiful part of the world and since my series started there, it seemed only right that it finish there also.

In *The Wedding Bargain*, Raif Masters has some big decisions to make. He already can't stand the groom, but should he help the woman he's crushed on for half of his life, especially when she's made it clear she wants no part of him? What should he do when the bride at the wedding he's reluctantly attending objects to her own marriage? And what of Shanal? Why did she agree to marry a man she clearly doesn't love and why is she running away now? I hope you enjoy finding the answers to these and other questions while reading *The Wedding Bargain*.

I love to hear from my readers. You can contact me via my website at yvonnelindsay.com or my Facebook page at facebook.com/yvonnelindsayauthor.

Best wishes and happy reading!

Yvonne Lindsay

THE WEDDING BARGAIN

———

YVONNE LINDSAY

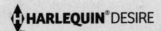
HARLEQUIN® DESIRE

Recycling programs
for this product may
not exist in your area.

ISBN-13: 978-0-373-73377-4

The Wedding Bargain

Printed in U.S.A.

A typical Piscean, *USA TODAY* bestselling author **Yvonne Lindsay** has always preferred her imagination to the real world. Married to her blind date hero and with two adult children, she spends her days crafting the stories of her heart, and in her spare time she can be found with her nose in a book reliving the power of love, or knitting socks and daydreaming. Contact her via her website: yvonnelindsay.com.

Books by Yvonne Lindsay

HARLEQUIN DESIRE

Wed at Any Price
Honor-Bound Groom
Stand-In Bride's Seduction
For the Sake of the Secret Child

The Master Vintners
The Wayward Son
A Forbidden Affair
One Secret Night
The High Price of Secrets
Wanting What She Can't Have
The Wedding Bargain

Visit the Author Profile page at Harlequin.com for more titles.

I don't often get the chance to tell my editor how much I appreciate her, but I want to do it here and now. E.M., you are amazing and I feel privileged to work with you.
Thank you for making my work shine.

One

"We are gathered here today..."

The priest's perfectly modulated voice filled the cathedral as sunlight filtered through the stained-glass windows, bathing the hallowed space with jeweled tones. The heady scent of the gardenias in Shanal's bridal bouquet, imported specifically at Burton's request, wafted up to fill her senses—and left her feeling slightly suffocated.

"...to join together Burton and Shanal in matrimony..."

Was this what she really wanted above all things? She looked across to her groom. Burton Rogers, so handsome, so intelligent, so successful. So rich. He was a good guy, no, a *great* guy. And she liked him, she really did.

Like. Such an insipid expression, really.

"...which is an honorable and solemn estate and

therefore is not to be entered into unadvisedly or lightly, but reverently and soberly."

Words she'd spoken to her best friend, Ethan Masters, only a year ago, echoed in her mind. *You have the chance to have the kind of forever love that many people can only dream of. I envy you that because that's the kind of love I want from the man I marry, if I ever marry. And you can be certain I'm not prepared to settle for less than that, ever.*

They'd been brave words, spoken before her world had begun to crumble around her. Before she'd chosen to sacrifice the chance to find true love. Before she'd latched onto the opportunity to give her parents a secure retirement after their lives had been torn apart.

Was Burton her forever love? No. Was she settling for less? Most definitely.

Everyone in the lab at the viticulture research center had said it had been a lucky day for her when she'd caught Burton's attention. They'd teased her about finding love in their clinical environment and she guessed, on the face of things, they had a point. As her boss, Burton had a reputation for expecting excellence in everything around him. Clearly, she had fallen within that category. And on the face of it, she'd agreed about how fortunate she was—faking joy amongst her colleagues when he'd proposed marriage and offered to solve her problems. She'd convinced everyone around her until she'd nearly believed herself that her engagement had made her the luckiest woman in the world.

Everyone gathered here in the cathedral believed this to be the happiest day of her life. Everyone except the one person who'd tried to talk her out of it. She flicked a glance sideways, but she couldn't spot Raif Masters, Ethan's cousin, in the crowd of two hundred guests jammed into the pews. She knew he was here, though. From the moment she'd walked down the aisle, accompanied by both her parents—her father in his wheelchair, on a rare appearance in public—she'd felt the simmering awareness that she felt only in Raif's presence.

"Into this estate these two persons present come now to be joined."

A buzzing sound began to build in Shanal's ears and her chest grew tight. A tremor in her hands made the heavy bouquet quiver—releasing another burst of cloying scent.

"If anyone here has just cause why Burton and Shanal may not be lawfully joined together, let them speak now or forever hold their peace."

Silence stretched out in the cathedral—silence filled with the ever increasing buzz in her ears and the erratic pounding of her heart.

Forever.

It was a very long time.

She thought for a brief second of her parents. Of how her father had always loved and provided for her mother. Of how her mother had always stood rock solid by her man, even now with all the uncertainty their future promised. Would Burton ever be that rock for her? Could he be? The priest's words echoed through her mind. *...just cause...not be lawfully joined together... speak now...*

"I do," Shanal said, her voice shaking, unsure.

Burton inclined his perfectly coiffed head, a puzzled twist to his lips. "Darling? That's not your line, not yet, anyway."

She dropped her bouquet, unheeding now of the scent of the flowers as they fell heavily on the carpeted altar, and worked her three-carat, princess-cut diamond engagement ring from her finger. A princess for his princess, Burton had said when he'd slid it on her hand—its fit perfect, of course.

Shanal thrust the ring toward him. "I can't do this, Burton. I'm so sorry," she choked out.

It was the first time she'd ever seen her erudite fiancé at a loss for words. With the perfect manners that were so much a part of him, he automatically accepted his ring back from her. The moment his fingers curled around the symbol of their future together, Shanal turned away from the priest in his raiment, her groom in his hand-finished tuxedo, and gathered her voluminous skirts in her hands.

"I'm sorry," she whispered in the direction of her parents, who sat in the front pew, their faces masks of shock, dismay and concern.

Then she ran.

Raif Masters had listened to the priest intoning the ceremony—a ceremony he was attending only as a favor to Ethan, who was away on his own honeymoon. Shanal Peat and Ethan had been friends for so long that it was almost as if she was part of the Masters family. It was only right that someone from the family be there for her today. He just wished it wasn't him. If Raif had had his way he'd have been anywhere but here. The idea of watching his cousin's best friend marrying Raif's nemesis was only slightly more appealing than spending the day passing a kidney stone.

He was already plotting his escape from the festivities at the earliest opportunity when he heard the objection request. He had, in fact, briefly considered standing up himself, because he did object to this wedding—on more than one level. But Shanal had made it perfectly clear a couple months ago that it wasn't his place to say anything. She hadn't wanted to hear it when he'd tried to explain to her that Burton Rogers was not the kind of man she should be tying herself to—literally or figuratively. Not for five minutes, let alone the rest of her life. But she had blinders on as far as Rogers was concerned, which, no doubt, was exactly as the other man liked it.

When Ethan had asked him to attend the wedding in his stead, Raif had objected quite emphatically, pointing out that he had no desire to see Rogers stand up to marry Shanal. In fact, he had no desire to see the other man, period. Even before the messiest parts of their history there had always been something about Burton that made Raif want to plant a fist in his arrogant face.

Ethan had brushed over his objections, reminding him that with all that was going on at The Masters, their family's resort and winery, he was the only one who could get away for the ceremony. Even so, it made Raif sick to his gut to see her willingly link herself to a man who lived by a single-minded agenda—doing whatever it took to make his life perfect, no matter who got hurt along the way. In Raif's experience, Burton was careless with others and only out for what he could get. He was the man Raif still held responsible for the death of his ex-girlfriend, Laurel Hollis, no matter what the coroner's findings had delivered.

Rogers had managed to walk away from the canyoneering accident without an ounce of blame, but while Raif hadn't been witness to it he had always believed there was more to the incident than had been disclosed. And he hadn't given up on finding out the truth one day, either. But for now, he had to sit and watch the woman he'd desired ever since he was a schoolboy with a crush that had lasted for longer than he cared to admit, marry a man he neither liked nor trusted.

Younger than her by three years, Raif had always found his relationship with Shanal awkward, right from when they'd first met fifteen years ago. Once she'd embarrassingly shattered his more intimate aspirations toward her—and in front of his entire family into the bargain—their interactions had been peppered with veiled barbs and verbal sparring when they'd crossed paths. But his attraction toward her had never dimmed, in spite of it all. And while they had never been close, he did truly care about her and wanted her to be happy.

He'd borne all that in mind when he'd gone to see her when the engagement was announced. Raif didn't believe that Burton Rogers was capable of making any woman lastingly happy, and had wanted to warn Shanal. He should have known better. Once she'd overcome her surprise at his visit, she hadn't hesitated to tell him he was wasting his time when he'd strongly urged her to reconsider her marriage to her boss. In fact she'd told him, with her usual economy with words, to butt out. And he had.

Now the entire cathedral was paralyzed in disbelief—Raif no less so than the people seated on the pew next to him.

Had his words been the catalyst that now sent her flying past him in a flurry of tulle and diamantes on her way down the aisle and out the front doors?

The stricken expression he'd spotted on her face galvanized him into action. Whatever their differences, she needed help. And since the reason she needed help was that she'd taken the advice *he* had given, he felt he owed it to her to be the one to come to her aid.

The doors of the church clanged closed in front of

him and he pulled one heavy wooden panel open and shot down the steps in hot pursuit of the vision in white that raced across the road without looking, and into the gardens beyond. That was where he found her— she'd stopped running by the time he caught up. Her breath was coming in great gasps and her usually glowing, light bronze skin now looked pale and sallow. Raif guided her to a bench and pushed her head down between her knees before she collapsed right there on the gravel path.

"Breathe," he instructed, ripping off his suit jacket and draping it over her bare, shaking shoulders, dwarfing her delicate frame. Adelaide in July was not warm, and dressed as she was in a strapless gown, she'd freeze in no time. "Slow and deep. C'mon," he said encouragingly. "You can do it."

"I…had…to get…away," she gasped.

He was shocked by how anxious she was. Shanal was always the Queen of Calm. Nothing unnerved her. Except maybe the carpet python he'd slipped in her bag when he was fifteen.

He rubbed her shoulders through the fine wool of his jacket. "Don't talk, just breathe, Shanal. It's going to be okay."

"No, no it's not."

Her words came out strangled, panicked.

"You'll work it out," he said, as reassuringly as he could under the circumstances.

Even as the words left his mouth he was reminded of the expression on Burton's face as he'd been left standing at the altar. An expression Shanal had missed seeing completely, thank God, or she might not have stopped running at all.

Raif had long known Burton was avaricious—he'd

always had to both *be* the best and *have* the best, by any means possible. But there was another edge to him, as well—and that edge had been clear on his face for a split second as he'd seen his latest intended acquisition flee from him. Raif might not have had much to do with him over the past three years, but he knew that Burton Rogers was not a man who enjoyed being thwarted.

Shanal struggled to sit upright, tugging flowers and her veil from her jet-black hair without any heed to the pins that must be raking her scalp. She tossed the destroyed blooms and filmy material to the walkway at her feet. She turned to Raif and grabbed his hands. He was shocked at how cold she felt already. As if she was chilled to her bones.

"Take me away," she implored. "Take me far away, right now."

It was the last thing he'd expected her to say.

"Are you sure?" he asked.

"Just, *please*, get me out of here," she begged, her bewitching, pale green eyes shining with unshed tears.

It was the tears that undid him. He thought about his Maserati, parked a good two blocks away. Only a handful of people had come out of the cathedral so far, but more were bound to follow soon. He and Shanal would never make it to the car before someone reached them, he thought, and once the crowd got to them, Shanal would be fielding questions left and right from a slew of concerned family members and friends wanting to know why she'd walked out on her own wedding. She didn't look as if she was up to conversation right now. As he swiftly considered their options, a taxi rounded the corner. Raif secured Shanal's small hand in his and pulled her to her feet.

"C'mon," he said, as he bolted for the sidewalk, towing Shanal along behind him.

He raised his hand to get the cabbie's attention. To his immense relief the guy pulled over, his eyes as round as saucers and his mouth hanging open as Raif yanked open the back door and guided Shanal inside. He barked his address to the startled driver as he yanked the door closed behind them.

Shanal sat next to him, pale but finally seeming more composed, as they pulled away from the curb and down the street. Raif cast one look through the back window. The crowd on the sidewalk outside the cathedral had grown. In its midst stood Burton, his eyes fixed on the retreating cab. Even from this distance Raif felt a prickle of unease. The groom, understandably, did not look happy.

Raif faced forward again. Burton's happiness had never been a priority of his, and as long as the man didn't take his anger out on Shanal in any way, Raif admitted to himself that he was delighted that his nemesis's day had been ruined.

He and Shanal had little privacy in the cab and Raif maintained his silence until, nearly forty-five minutes later, they reached his home. His phone, already on Silent for the ceremony, vibrated continuously in his trouser pocket. He knew exactly who was calling—and he had no intention of answering him.

"What are we doing here?" Shanal asked as the cab drew away, leaving them outside Raif's single-level home nestled at the edge of the family's old and well-established vineyard. "It's the first place he'll look, isn't it? He's bound to have seen us getting into the cab together."

Raif's eyebrows shot up. "I hadn't realized we were

meant to be hiding from him. You really don't want him to know where you are? You're absolutely certain you don't want to work this out with him?"

In response, Shanal shuddered. "No, I can't. I...I just can't."

Raif reached past her to unlock his front door, then gestured for her to precede him. The incongruity of the situation struck him. He'd always imagined bringing a bride back here to his home one day—just not exactly like this. But if she wanted to get away from Burton, then the least Raif could do was let her freshen up before she headed off to...wherever it was she planned on going from here.

"Can I get you something to drink?"

"Some water, please."

She followed him into the open-plan living area, her heels clicking and the multilayered skirts of her gown making a swooshing sound on the hard surface of the tiled floor. In the kitchen, he poured her a glass of mineral water from the fridge and handed it to her. She took a long drink.

"Thanks," she said, putting the glass down on the granite countertop with a click. "I needed that. Now where are you taking me? We can't stay here."

Taking her? What made her think he was taking her anywhere? She'd asked him to get her away from the wedding. He'd done that. Surely that was where his involvement began and ended. Not that he was unwilling to help her, but she'd always been so aloof toward him, had always kept him very firmly at a distance. Why would she be depending on him now? It was so unlike her.

Shanal obviously realized what he was thinking. "I'm

sorry, that was presumptuous of me. What I meant was, can you help me to get away for a bit? I'm kind of stuck."

She held her arms out from her dress in a gesture of helplessness. She was right. She was stuck, and in what she was wearing right now. She didn't even have a purse with her.

Raif studied her carefully. Her face was stretched into a tight mask of strain and her eyes had the look of a frightened animal. Even though this shouldn't be his problem right now, he racked his brains for something he could do to help her—somewhere she could go to get away from this whole mess. Ethan had chosen a fine time to marry his long-time fiancée, Isobel, and head away on a honeymoon cruise in the Caribbean, Raif thought uncharitably. A smile twisted one side of his mouth as an idea bloomed in his mind.

"How about a cruise?"

"A cruise?" Shanal looked surprise.

"Yeah. On a riverboat. I have a friend who has just re-engined and refurbished one of his fleet. He was moaning about not having time to run the motor in before it gets repositioned farther up the Murray. A nice, slow trip up the river sounds like just what you need and you'd be doing Mac a favor by getting some hours on the engine, as well."

"How soon can we leave?"

"You're serious? You want to do that?"

She nodded.

"Let me make a call."

He stepped out of the living area and into his office on the other side of the hall. He checked his phone. Yup, there were several messages, most of them from the same number—Burton Rogers. He deleted those without listening. Let the guy simmer in his own juices for a while. He frowned a little when he recognized Shanal's parents' number. He'd have to let them know she was okay, but first he needed to contact his friend.

Now, where had he put Mac's contact details... Aha! Raif spied the business card his friend had given him when they'd last caught up for a drink in Adelaide, and keyed the number into his phone. A few minutes later it was all set.

Shanal was standing at the large bifold glass doors that faced the vineyard when he came back into the room. She'd slid his jacket off her shoulders and had pulled the last of the pins from her hair, leaving it to cascade down her back like a long, wavy black river of silk. His hand itched to reach out, to touch her hair, to stroke it. Stupid, he told himself. The persistent physical attraction that had ignited back when he was a schoolboy continued to simmer beneath the surface, but he knew better than to act on it. Shanal herself had taught him that lesson. He'd gotten this far through his life without setting himself up for another smackdown like the one she'd dealt him twelve years ago, and he certainly wasn't going to set himself up for one now.

"You okay?" he asked.

She sighed, her body wilting from its strong stance. She shook her head. "No, I'm not. I don't think I'm ever going to be okay after this."

"Hey, of course you will. I've spoken to Mac and he's happy to make the boat available. With the school holidays over it's pretty quiet for him right now, so you can take all the time you need. It'll be good for you, the perfect getaway. You'll have time and space to think, and when you come back you can tackle what happens next with a fresh mind."

Her lips twisted into a semblance of a smile. "Somehow I don't think a fresh mind is going to make a big difference in resolving my problems, but thank you for all you've done. How soon can we leave?"

Raif calculated. It was just over an hour's drive to Mannum, where Mac would have the houseboat waiting.

"I'll need to get changed first. Do you want me to see if Cathleen left anything here that you can change into? We can always pick you up some more clothes on the way to the marina if you like."

His younger sister had house-sat for him when he'd gone to France on a recent fact-finding mission relating to the family vineyard operations. Not that the place needed to be minded, but while Cathleen for the most part loved living with the rest of their family at The Masters, when the opportunity to be on her own arose from time to time, she clutched at it with both hands. He could understand why she felt like that. It was, after all, why he'd chosen to build here, on the fringe of the family's oldest vineyard, as opposed to taking a suite of rooms in the family home. Sometimes a person just needed to be alone.

"Please," Shanal said, plucking at the skirts of her gown. "I really want to get out of this. It's a little attention seeking, don't you think?"

It was good to see she still had a touch of the acerbic humor he'd borne the brunt of so often in the past.

"A little," he agreed with a quirk of his lips. "Come with me and let's see what we can find."

He led her down the hall toward the guest wing of the house and to the room Cathleen had used. There, he slid open one of the wardrobe doors. For the first time ever he silently thanked his sister for her habit of leaving her things wherever she went. A clean pair of jeans and some tops were neatly folded on a shelf in the wardrobe. A lightweight jacket hung on the rail and there was even a pair of sneakers in a box on the floor.

"You two are about the same size, aren't you?" he said, gesturing to the garments in the cupboard.

"Close." Shanal nodded and reached for the jeans and one of the long-sleeved T-shirts, which she put on the bed behind them. "But even if the clothes aren't a perfect fit, given the circumstances, I'd rather wear anything else than this dress. Can you help me get out of it? The buttons are so tiny I can't do it on my own."

Raif swallowed against the dryness that suddenly hit his throat. Undress her? Hell, he'd dreamed about this moment on and off since he was fifteen years old. He slammed the door on his wayward thoughts. This was neither the time nor the place to indulge in his fantasies, he informed himself firmly. She needed a friend right now, and that was what he'd be. Nothing more. Now and always, she didn't want anything more from him—and he wasn't going to set himself up for yet another rejection from her.

Shanal turned her back to him and lifted the swathe of her hair to one side. A waft of her fragrance, an intoxicating blend of spice and flowers, enticed him. Urged him to dip his head and inhale more deeply. He fought the impulse and breathed through his mouth. She wasn't his to touch, or taste, *or anything*, he reminded himself.

She'd just run from her fiancé, and while every cell in his body was thrilled to bits about that—some cells more than others—he wasn't the kind of guy to take advantage of it. Not out of any respect for Burton, because the man deserved nothing but his contempt. But for Shanal's sake. Whatever had driven her to leave her wedding in the middle of the ceremony—and in the back of his mind he ached to know what it was that had triggered her last-minute change of heart—she was clearly shaken and upset. Unwanted attentions from a guy she'd rejected a dozen times over were the last thing she needed.

Raif took in a deep breath, then applied himself to his task. Shanal's skin was a delicate bronze above the edge of her strapless dress. A color that signaled the mixed heritage of her Indian mother and Australian dad.

"I'm surprised you didn't wear a sari," Raif commented, determined to distract her from the fact that his fingers, usually dexterous and quite capable of the job at hand, had become uncharacteristically clumsy in the face of her proximity and the way that the tiny buttons, undone one by one, revealed more of her beautiful skin.

His fingers slipped on a button, brushing against her. Her skin peppered with goose bumps and he heard her gasp.

"Sorry," he said, forcing himself to take more care.

"It's okay," she said, her voice a little husky. "And as to your question about the sari? Burton said he preferred me to dress more traditionally."

Raif frowned and was unable to keep the irritation from his voice when he spoke. "Traditionally? For whom?"

Shanal didn't answer his question. "I think I can manage the rest myself," she said, stepping just slightly out of his reach and pressing her hands against the crystal-encrusted bodice of her gown to stop it from sliding farther down. "Thank you."

"No problem. I'll be down the hall getting changed myself. Just holler if you need me."

Her pale eyes met his and he felt her trust in him as if it was a tangible thing. It was a surprisingly heady feeling. Shanal had always been so cool, so untouchable and in control. He'd never seen her this vulnerable, and the fact that she chose to put her trust in Raif when her guard was down… It meant a lot.

She gave him a small nod, then collected Cathleen's clothes off the bed and turned to the bathroom. "I won't be too long."

"Take as long as you need," he said, and left the room. *In fact, take longer*, he added silently. Because it sure as hell was going to take him a while to get his raging hormones under control.

Two

Shanal closed the bathroom door behind her and stripped away her wedding dress. Without caring about any possible damage to the delicate and expensive fabric, she let it drop to the floor. She shuddered. Right now she felt so cold, deep down into her bones.

She quickly tugged on the jeans and sucked her tummy in a little to do up the zipper. Cathleen's curves were just a bit more subtle than her own and it showed in the cut of jeans that she favored. Too bad, Shanal thought as she slid her arms into the sleeves of the T-shirt and pulled it over her head. Beggars couldn't be choosers. That final thought held a painful irony she didn't want to think about right now. She had enough on her plate.

There was still an air of unreality about what she'd just done. In fact, she could barely believe she'd done it. Run away from everything—everyone.

Burton would be angry, she knew. Justifiably so?

Very likely. They'd had an agreement, and if she'd
learned anything about Burton Rogers it was that he
couldn't bear to be thwarted, not to mention being hu-
miliated in front of a cathedral packed with his peers.
She certainly wasn't in any headspace to face that right
now.

It wasn't that she was worried he'd get physical with
his rage—no, that would be beneath his dignity—but
how did you explain to a man, especially one who on
the surface was every woman's dream, that you no longer wanted to be his bride? All she knew was that she
couldn't go through with it. She needed space—time
to think, to form a strategy to overcome this situation
she'd put herself into.

Another shudder ran through her and she felt her
chest constrict anew. Her breathing became difficult
again and she closed her eyes and focused on one breath
in, one long breath out. When the tightness began to
ease, she reached for the logical side of her brain. The
one that had weighed the options of Burton's offer of
marriage so carefully and had accepted it, knowing
she didn't love him. The tension returned twofold. No,
she couldn't even think about it. She felt so close to
the breaking point. The two people who now depended
upon her most, her mum and her dad, would be beside
themselves with worry. For her. For themselves. Her
father's medical expenses aside, in a few months they
would be struggling to meet paying their utilities, let
alone affording the basics like food.

Her decision to run away from Burton would af-
fect them all.

She'd find a way around it. She had to. The alternative simply wasn't an option. And maybe it wouldn't
be so bad, after all—maybe it was just her panicked

mind that was making it seem worse than she thought. Right now, though, she needed distance. Distance *and* a healthy dose of perspective. Raif had offered her both unquestioningly.

But what was his angle? Was he doing this because he wanted to help her—or just because he wanted to hurt Burton? He'd come to see her at her parents' home three months ago after her engagement had been announced. He hadn't wasted time on niceties such as saying congratulations. He'd come straight to the point and said he was there to talk her out of marrying Burton. She'd told him the wedding would go ahead no matter what he had to say, and had very firmly asked him to leave, without hearing him out. She knew there was bad blood between him and Burton; she'd gotten the sense from what Burton had said that it had been some idiotic male rivalry over a woman. Whatever had happened, Raif had clearly carried a grudge, and she'd assumed that was what had motivated him to see her.

A deep and painful throbbing started behind her eyes. It was all too much to think about. Right now she felt as if she could simply crawl under the covers of the bed in the room next door and go to sleep for a week. Instead, she forced herself to move and put on a pair of socks and the shoes Cathleen had left behind.

When Shanal looked up into the mirror, her reflection was that of a stranger. She never usually wore this much makeup—hadn't really wanted to, even today— but Burton had insisted she allow him to send along a makeup artist during her preparations on the morning of their *special* day. She'd acquiesced, thinking it didn't matter, but as each layer of cosmetics had been applied she'd felt as if her true self was being hidden.

As if pieces of her were being pushed further and further into obscurity.

Was that what it would be like being married to Burton? His decisions overriding hers and suffocating everything that defined her until her very identity was buried beneath what *he* wanted? She bent over the bathroom basin and scrubbed her face clean, desperate to grab that part of herself back again.

A knock at the door turned her mind willingly away from questions she couldn't face and didn't want to answer.

"You okay?" she heard Raif ask through the door.

No, she was not okay. Not right now. But she had to hope she would be. "You can come in," she answered.

He did, and she noticed he'd changed into a pair of well-worn jeans that hugged his hips, and a navy sweater. The fisherman's rib knit clung to his broad shoulders, making him look impossibly strong and masculine. As if he could take on the weight of the world and barely notice the strain. She certainly hoped that was the case, because at this moment she felt even closer to fracturing apart than she had half an hour ago.

"We should hit the road. I've loaded up a bag in the Jeep with some things for you. Clothes of mine you can borrow—y'know, track pants, sweaters and a thicker jacket than that one of Cathleen's. They'll be far too big for you, but at least you'll be warm. We can stop somewhere and get you some underwear, toiletries and anything else you think of, on the way through."

She nodded. It was such a relief to simply hand over her care to him. To have someone else do all the thinking for a change. Shanal followed him out of the room, not even sparing a glance for the mound of tulle that still lay on the bathroom floor.

"I need to call my parents," she said as they reached the door to the garage. "To let them know I'm okay."

"Already done," Raif answered smoothly. "They send their love."

Did they? Or did they send their recriminations, their fears for the future now that she'd dashed their only hope for a secure retirement? The financial settlement Burton had agreed to pay her on their marriage would never happen now—in fact, she probably wouldn't even have a job after this.

"Are…are they all right?"

"They're worried about you, but I assured them you're being cared for."

She swallowed a sob and murmured a response, but something in her tone made Raif whip his head around and study her carefully.

"It'll be okay, Shanal. You did the right thing."

But had she? Or had she simply destroyed not only her parents' future, but her own, as well? Raif opened the passenger door of the Jeep for her to climb up before he walked around to the other side.

"Mac is stocking the houseboat with everything you'll need for a week, at least," Raif said as he settled in the driver's seat and hit the remote for the garage door.

"I'll pay you back, Raif. I promise," she said brokenly.

"Don't worry about that right now," he replied. "Why don't you put your seat back a bit and close your eyes. You look done in. Try and get a little sleep, huh?"

She did as he suggested, but found her mind was too active to sleep. Instead she listened as he called his younger brother, Cade, and arranged for him to collect the car that Raif had left parked near the church. Guilt sliced deep as she considered everything he had done for her so far today. And now he was going out of his way to drive her all the way to Mannum so she could take time out.

For someone she'd never exactly treated well, he seemed to be prepared to go to great lengths for her. Maybe it was just a measure of the man he was, she thought, as she heard him laughingly warn his sibling not to drive the Maserati too fast through the Adelaide hills on the way to his property. A man who, she had to admit to herself, she didn't know very well at all. When he ended the call he turned on the radio, tuned to a classical-music station. She was surprised, thinking him more likely to be into popular music or rock than anything resembling culture.

But then again, what did she really know about him aside from the fact that he was her best friend's cousin? Sure, he'd always been there when Ethan had invited her to attend family functions at The Masters. But Raif was three years younger than her and back when she'd met him, that three-year age gap between him at fifteen and her at eighteen going on nineteen had seemed huge. She'd mentally filed him away as a child, and had barely given him a second thought.

She'd recognized he had a crush on her early on, but had ignored it—and him, too, for the most part. He had been easy enough to ignore at first, especially since their paths didn't cross all that often. When she thought of him even now, she tended to think of the child he had been. Shanal hadn't really noticed when he'd left childhood behind for good.

Until now.

Until she'd realized the boy had most definitely

grown into a man. A man she could depend upon when it seemed she had no other options available to her.

She opened her eyes and watched him as he drove, his concentration on the road ahead, his hands capable and sure on the wheel. He was a bit more leanly built than Ethan, but aside from that the family resemblance was strong. Just over six feet tall, with dark hair brushed back off his forehead and blue eyes that always seemed to notice far too much, Raif, like the rest of the Masters family had more than his fair share of good-looking DNA. Added to that was the perpetual tan he wore, a byproduct of his work outdoors on the vines that grew in the various vineyards run by The Masters. But even so, the differences were there if you looked hard enough. There was a suppressed energy about Raif, whereas his cousin was calm and measured in everything he did. Raif projected a more physical and active air.

There was no doubt he was a man who thrived on action and on thinking on his feet. His spontaneity was one of the reasons it had been so easy to continue thinking of him as the child he'd once been—impulsive and thoughtless, never considering the consequences. Today had been a perfect example of that. What was it that Ethan often said about Raif? Ah, yes, he was the kind of guy to always leap before he looked. Well, today she was truly thankful for that. Not at any stage had he asked her why she'd run from her wedding. He'd simply taken her away when she'd begged to be taken.

If it weren't for him, she had no idea where she'd be or what she'd be doing. She was *not* the impulsive type, and never had been. Every choice was always meticulously planned and carefully considered. Until today. When she'd run out of that cathedral, she'd had no plan in mind, no destination in her sights. She'd just wanted to get *away*, with no thought for what would come next. Thank goodness Raif had run after her when he did. He might not be someone she thought of as a white knight, but he'd certainly come to her rescue. And the certainty that he had the situation in hand for the time being was enough to let her relax. For now, at least.

A steady rain began to fall and Raif switched on the windshield wipers. The rhythmic *clack-swish* of the blades across the glass was soothing and Shanal let her eyes close again, barely even aware that she was drifting off into sleep. When she awoke she found she was alone in the car. She struggled upright and rubbed her neck to ease the kinks out. Looking around, Shanal couldn't identify exactly where they were, but she spotted Raif exiting a small grocery store across the road. As he got back in the car he tossed a plastic bag in her direction.

"I didn't want to wake you so I guessed your size."

She opened the sack and spied a six-pack of multi-colored cotton panties and some ladies' toiletries inside. A blush bloomed in her cheeks at the thought of him choosing her underwear, but she pushed it aside. She should be grateful he was being practical about things.

"Thanks, it looks like you guessed right. And thank you again for helping me today. I—I don't know what I'd have done without you."

Emotion threatened to swamp her, and she felt his warm strong fingers close over one of her hands. A surprising tingle of response made her pull away. He gave her a sharp look.

"No problem," he said steadily. "Are you hungry yet?"

She should be enjoying the sumptuous repast that

had been booked at the reception center. Her stomach twisted. She couldn't think of anything less appealing.

"I'm okay for now. How about you?"

"I can wait," he said calmly as he started up the Jeep and swung back onto the road.

"Are we far from the river?" she asked.

"About ten minutes."

True to his word, they pulled up at a small marina a short while later. The rain had stopped, but there was a cool wind blowing, and Shanal wrapped her arms around herself as they got out of the vehicle. She should have grabbed that jacket of Cathleen's back at the house.

"Here, put this on."

She caught the down-filled jacket Raif tossed toward her from the back of the Jeep, and gratefully slid her arms inside. Instantly, she began to feel the warmth, almost as if he'd closed his arms around her and given her the comfort she so desperately craved today. She followed him in silence to the pier where a man waited for them.

"Mac, this is my friend Shanal."

Mac nodded a grizzled head in her direction. "Come aboard, I'll show you around."

Shanal was surprised by the luxury of the fittings on board. The boat, apparently one of Mac's smallest, boasted three bedrooms and was more spacious than the compact town house she'd rented back in Adelaide before having to move home to help her parents. In fact, the layout was similar, the only major differences being the helm positioned near the dining area of the boat's large main entertainment cabin, and the fact they were floating on the river.

"You driven one of these before?" Mac asked.

"No, but I'm sure Raif will show me."

"Better you get Mac to show you now," Raif said. "You'll need to know what to do when you're out on the water."

She noticed he didn't make mention of "we." Shanal turned troubled eyes to him and fresh panic clawed at her throat. "You're not coming with me?"

"Give us a minute," Raif said to Mac, before drawing Shanal onto the deck at the front of the boat.

He was shocked to feel her trembling beneath his touch. She'd appeared calmer after that nap she'd taken in the car, and some of the shell-shocked look in her eyes had faded, but it was back again now, with interest.

"Here," he said, pulling out one of the iron chairs that matched the glass-topped dining table on the deck. "Sit down."

He squatted in front of her, taking both her hands and chafing them between his. He was worried at how icy cold she felt to his touch.

"I thought you'd be coming, too. You're not going to leave me, are you?" she whispered.

Raif studied her, taking in the blatant plea in her beautiful green eyes and the worried frown that pulled between her brows. He hadn't planned to go with her. Honestly, it had never occurred to him that she'd want him there with her. All he'd done today was remove her from a bad situation and organize the escape she had wanted. He hadn't imagined she'd have any use for him beyond that.

And yet everything he knew about who she was—how strong and intelligent, how confident and admired—seemed to crumble before his eyes as he looked at her now. He'd thought the houseboat would be the ideal opportunity for her to get away and to think—to get things straight in her mind again before she went back to face the music. Why would she want him there for that? Why would she want any man around her when she'd just left her intended groom at the altar?

Though this was a woman who, in his experience at least, had no qualms about publicly humiliating men. Witness his own embarrassment when, in front of his entire family, she'd laughingly spurned his attempts to ask her to his high school graduation dance all those years ago. The sting of embarrassment had hurt far more than he'd ever admitted. Granted, it wasn't on par with what she'd done to Burton, but her method of making clear she wasn't interested had a way of staying with a guy.

"I'm sorry," she said, interrupting his thoughts. "I'm asking for more when you've already done so much for me. It's just…" She worried at her lower lip with her teeth and her gaze slipped out over the river that stretched before them.

"It's just?" he prompted.

"I don't want to be alone," she whispered, her words so quietly spoken.

The sudden vulnerability in her voice, hell, in her entire body, hit him fair and square in the solar plexus. Her slender fingers closed around his.

"You've already packed a bag," she said in a lame attempt at humor before becoming all serious again. "Raif, please? I know this is a big favor for me to ask, but I really need to be with someone I can trust right now. Just while I work things out."

She trusted him? Well, he wished he could say the feeling was mutual, but he certainly didn't trust her. During the drive here he'd had more time to think. When he'd talked to her after her engagement, she'd been so adamant that the wedding would go ahead. He doubted that anything *he'd* tried to say back then had been the trigger to change her mind. She'd certainly never before given his thoughts or feelings any weight in the choices she'd made. So what had changed things for her? She had to be holding something back, perhaps the very something that had put the haunted look in her eyes.

He considered her plea, turning it over in his mind. He wasn't prepared for this. Still, what harm would it do? Working the viticulture side of the family business certainly had its advantages come wintertime in that things definitely slowed down for him once he'd finished winter cane pruning on the vineyard. There was no other pressing business holding him at The Masters, nothing to prevent him from taking a week off work, if that's the time it took for Shanal to ready herself to face the world again. Besides, there were three bedrooms on the boat.

Movement in the cabin caught his attention. Mac was getting fidgety, casting them a curious glance every now and then. Raif had to make a decision. Leave her to her own devices, or go with her. He knew what Ethan would do. More importantly, what Ethan would expect *him* to do.

Sometimes family honor was a bitch.

"Fine," he said with a huff of breath. "I'll come with you."

Three

Relief swamped her and she put out her hands to grasp his.

"Thank you. I owe you so much already—"

Raif pulled away from her and stood up. "You don't owe me anything."

She felt his withdrawal as if it was a slap. She lifted a hand to her throat as she watched him go back inside the main cabin. God, she'd made such a mess of all this. Did he regret rescuing her today? She wouldn't blame him if he did. It was one thing to whisk her away from the scene of her shattered future, quite another to continue on the journey with her. She was asking such a lot from him. And it wasn't as if they'd ever been close.

Aware of his crush on her, she'd always made a point of keeping her distance, never doing anything to lead him on. She'd felt that in the long run, that was the kinder choice—though admittedly, that had been as much for her sake as for his. Ever since he'd transitioned from schoolboy to young man, there had been something about Raif that had made the hairs on the back of her neck stand to attention. Something indefinable that always put her on edge when he was around, and that made her uncomfortably aware of herself and her body's reactions to him.

She'd told herself way back then that it was ridiculous. She had her whole life planned out, and someone like Raif had no place in it. He already had that devil-may-care attitude to life, while she was always quieter, more considered in her decisions. They'd had nothing in common whatsoever aside from Ethan as a link.

But that had been nearly a decade ago. A lot had changed, for both of them, since then. He'd become fully a man, and was now even more confident, more self-assured, with that air of entitlement and power that all the Masters men effortlessly exuded. And she? Well, she was still that nerd with her nose in her research, and she was no less discomfited by his presence than she'd ever been.

That moment back at his house, when his fingertips had touched her spine, had felt electric. All her nerve endings had jittered with the shock of it—and now the two of them would be confined together for the better part of the next few days. She started to wonder if she'd made a mistake in asking him to stay.

From inside, she could hear Raif's deep voice as he talked to Mac. Soon after, the two men hugged briefly and Mac debarked. Raif assumed his position at the helm and started up the engine. Mac cast them off from the pier with a wave. As the boat eased into the murky river waters, swollen with recent winter rain, Shanal felt a little of the tension that gripped her body begin to ease. She rose from the chair and went inside.

"I guess this has put a spanner in everything for you," she said, as Raif met her gaze.

His broad shoulders lifted in a nonchalant shrug. "It's not a problem. I'll let the family know I'll be away for a few days, and besides, I have nothing more important to deal with right now."

She felt the slight in his words—the implication that she was no more than a minor irritation to be dealt with—and stifled a sigh. "You're probably wondering why I ran away."

Again, that casual lift of his shoulders. "Not my business."

She struggled to find the words to begin to tell him. To explain her sudden overwhelming sense of suffocation and irrational fear. Standing at the altar—was it only a couple of hours ago?—and listening to the priest had forced her to see the rest of her life stretching out before her. None of it being as she'd planned.

Sure, as Burton's wife she'd still be heavily involved in her research—finding refuge in facts and figures and analysis—and she'd finally hold the position she'd craved for years. When it had come to negotiating their prenuptial agreement—a clinical document designed to appoint Shanal as head of research within the facility and to outline the terms of the large monetary settlement to be made to her upon their marriage—she'd had one thing only on her mind. Security. Not happiness. Not love—well, except for the love she bore for her parents, and her desire to lift the strain and sorrow from her father's frail shoulders for the life he had left.

While everything had been under discussion and was being fine-tuned by their legal counsel, it had seemed to be a reasonable trade-off. Financial security for her parents and job security for herself in exchange for marriage to a handsome, wealthy, charming man who she simply didn't happen to love. But perhaps love would come later, she had thought at the time.

Burton had made no secret of his attraction to her from the day she'd started working at the research facility that bore his name. They'd had the occasional date now and then. Nothing serious—or so she'd thought. But then he'd surprised her with his proposal of marriage. Shanal had avoided giving him an answer straightaway, certain that she'd have to tell him no, but wary of what her refusal might do for her chances of advancement within Burton International. But then her mother had taken her aside one day and disclosed the dire position that she and Shanal's father were in.

Shanal knew that the medical-negligence claim against her dad about five years back had cost him heavily. A proud man, proud in particular of his skill and sterling reputation as a physician, he'd hidden the early symptoms of motor neuron disease, to his cost and, even worse, to the cost of the life of one of his patients. After that dreadful episode, he'd been forced to give up his cardiovascular practice. No one wanted a surgeon whose muscles were systematically wasting away, leading to unexpected twitching. And certainly no one wanted a man who'd let his pride stand in the way of someone's life.

His malpractice insurance had covered some of the costs of the suit that had been brought against him. But bowed by guilt, and with his funds tied up in long-term investments that were time-consuming and expensive to convert into cash, her father had taken out a short-term loan to make a large private financial settlement on the family of his deceased patient. Using his home as security had seemed a good idea at the time, and he'd had every intention of paying the loan back out of investment income. Until the truth about his investments had been revealed.

He'd trusted his old school friend who ran a financial-planning company. A friend who had, unfortunately, turned out to be running an intricate Ponzi scheme. Shanal's parents had lost every last dollar. Shanal had given up her rental and moved back home immediately to help them out.

While she earned a good salary and had some savings, she knew it wouldn't support the three of them forever. For the time being, they were able to afford the loan payments and living expenses, but those expenses would soon rise beyond what she could handle, especially as her father's disease took greater hold on his body and he grew more dependent upon assistance. It struck Shanal as cruelly ironic that while her father had paid dearly to buy security for his patient's family, everyone in his own was now paying for it.

In a weak moment she'd shared her worries with Burton, who'd immediately proposed marriage again, saying he'd planned to make her his wife all along and that the timing was perfect now, since as her husband, he'd be able to help her and her family. For starters, he'd insisted on taking over her parents' mortgage and offering a financial settlement to relieve her and her parents' stress when they married. She had honestly believed she could go through with it.

The reality, however, had been an unwelcome shock. Once she'd agreed to become his wife, Burton had shown himself to be intent on taking over much more than just her parents' mortgage. The overwhelming sense of loss of self that had struck her when she'd been standing at the altar still lingered like cold, bony fingers plucking at her heart—at her mind. She closed her eyes briefly and shook her head to try and rid herself of the sensation.

When she opened them, Raif was looking at her again with those piercing blue eyes. She felt as if he looked right through her, but at the same time couldn't *see* what twisted and tormented her inside. She wanted to break free of that gaze—to do something, anything, to keep herself busy, even if only for a couple minutes.

"I'll make us some coffee, shall I?" she said, her voice artificially bright.

"Sure. Black for me."

Of course his coffee would be black. Deceptively simple, like the man himself, yet with hidden depths and nuances at the same time. Shanal familiarized herself with the well-appointed kitchen, finding the coffeemaker and mugs tucked neatly away.

"How long have you known Mac?" she asked, determined to fill the silence that spread out between them.

"About five years."

She waited for him to be more forthcoming, but may as well have been waiting for the polar caps to melt.

"How did you meet?" she persisted.

"We did some skydiving together, some canyoneering."

Shanal was well aware of Raif's interest in adventure sports. For a while it had seemed he was always hurling himself off some high peak or out some airplane, or kayaking down a wild river. The activities seemed a perfect match for the man he was—physical, daring and impulsive. But Raif's interest in such activities had waned suddenly after the death of his girlfriend, Laurel, in a canyoneering accident a few years ago.

"Did he know Laurel?" Shanal blurted, without really thinking.

"She was his daughter."

"Oh." Her hands shook as she went to put her standard spoonful of sugar in her mug, and the white granules scattered over the kitchen counter. "I'm sorry. I didn't mean to bring that up."

"It's okay," he replied, his voice gruff. "I don't mind talking about her."

Shanal flicked him a glance, noted the way his hands had tightened on the wheel, his knuckles whitening. "That's the hard thing about losing someone, isn't it? People often don't know what to say, so they say nothing at all."

Raif grunted a noncommittal response. Shanal finished making the coffee, thinking about what she'd said. She'd discovered the same thing applied when people suffered other tragedies—like illness. No one really wanted to face the issue, and conversation usually skirted around things. At least that's what she'd found with her father. As the motor neuron disease ravaged his body, piece by piece, he'd lost his independence and ability. Their friends, not knowing what to do or how to help, had slowly withdrawn.

It hadn't helped that her dad was such a proud and private man. He'd hated being forced into retirement because of his illness—still hated every lost ability, every task that he could no longer complete on his own that forced him to depend on the care of others. He had always taken such pride in his independence, his abilities. His work as a surgeon had saved lives and allowed him to provide handsomely for his family in a way that gave him a sense of purpose and meaning. Losing all that had been devastating. He'd become reclusive, despising himself for his growing dependency on others.

And then there was the financial situation.

Shanal slammed the door on her thoughts before guilt could overwhelm her. She had, literally, run away from the answer to her parents' financial problems. She didn't want to go down that road right now. She just couldn't. Maybe in a few days a solution would present itself to her—and maybe vines would one day grow grapes of solid gold, she thought, deriding herself.

She handed Raif his coffee and sat down beside him as he negotiated the boat up the river.

"How far do you plan to go today?"

"Not far," he replied, before taking a sip. "The sun will be setting in a couple of hours. We can pick a spot along the river, tie off for the night and then make an early start tomorrow if you feel like it."

"Sounds good to me."

"Here," he said. "Do you want to have a turn at the wheel?"

"Is that safe? I've never done this before."

"Gotta start somewhere," he replied. "Besides, we're not doing more than seven kilometers an hour. I don't think even you could get us into trouble at this speed."

"You're referring to the time I crashed one of the vineyard tractors into the side of a shed, aren't you?"

His lips quirked.

"In my defense, no one told me where the brake was on that thing."

"Point taken. Which brings us to your first lesson today."

He briefly explained the controls in front of them and then let her take the wheel. Once she got the hang of it, Shanal found it surprisingly relaxing as she gently guided the boat along the river.

The sun was getting low in the sky, sending the last of its watery golden rays through the trees silhouetted on the riverbank, when Raif suggested they pull in at a tiny beach on the river's edge. After they'd nosed in, and he'd set up the small gangplank, he went ashore to tie ropes to a couple of large tree stumps. Shanal shut down the motor, as instructed, and walked out onto the front deck.

"I know this is crazy," she said. "But I feel as if we're the only people on the river right now."

"I know what you mean. You get a sense of isolation very quickly out here. It's good in its way."

"Thank you. I really did need this."

He dipped his head in acknowledgment and went inside. After a few minutes she followed. Raif was opening a bottle of wine at the kitchen counter.

"Want some?" he asked, holding up an empty glass.

"Yes, please."

She watched as he poured the white wine, and accepted the glass when he handed it to her.

"Yours?" she asked.

"Of course. My grapes, Ethan's brilliance."

She smiled. "You make a good pair."

"Just like our dads did before us."

"Is your dad still hands-on in the vineyard?"

Raif took a sip of the wine and made a sound of appreciation. "Yeah, although he's pulling back more these days. He and Mum are planning a tour of Alsace and Bordeaux next year. He's been tied to the vineyard for most of his adult life. It'll be good for them to explore a bit more, and I know they'll love France."

Shanal took a sip of her wine, savoring the flavor

as it burst over her tongue. "This is from the vineyard by your house, isn't it? The one that partially survived the big fire?"

The Masters family had been devastated just over thirty years ago, when bush fires had destroyed the family residence, Masters Rise, and almost all their vineyards. It had taken years for them to recover. Years and many hours of hard work and determination from a family that had pulled together, growing closer and more unified in the face of the tragedy. Now, they were successful and strong again, but the ruins of the old house still stood sentinel over the family property—a solemn reminder that everything could be snatched away in the blink of an eye.

"Certainly is," Raif confirmed.

"Ethan was telling me that you've become a keen proponent of organic vineyard practices."

He smiled at that—the first real smile she'd seen from him all day—and seemed to relax a bit. "It's hard to break with the old ways, but I think in this case it's worthwhile. It's always been my aim to work toward making the vineyards as efficient as possible using sustainable processes."

"Well, if this vintage is any example, you're definitely on the right track."

He held his glass up in a silent acknowledgment of her compliment. "Shall we take these outside? You'll be warm enough if you put my jacket back on."

Shanal followed his suggestion, and after putting on the jacket she'd discarded on the couch earlier, walked out onto the front deck and sat in one of the wicker easy chairs positioned there. The sun gave a final burst of golden color before disappearing. Darkness spread, heightening the sense of isolation she'd mentioned earlier. And yet even with the night's noises beginning around them, she didn't feel anxious or afraid. Raif's solid presence beside her put paid to that, she realized. And no wonder she felt safe with him, given the way he'd helped and protected her today. She owed him, big time. Not many men would have done what he did.

She sighed and sipped her wine. The silence between them was companionable, but she felt compelled to say something about the way she'd absconded from her own wedding.

"I guess I owe you an explanation," she started, turning to face Raif, who stared out into the darkness beside her.

"Nope."

Raif had no need to know what had finally brought Shanal to her senses and sent her flying from the cathedral this morning. And frankly, the less time they spent talking about her would-be groom, the better Raif would feel.

"But I—"

"Look," he interrupted. "Burton Rogers and I might have been at school together. We might even have resembled friends once upon a time, but we're not now. To be honest, I've wondered more about your reasons for agreeing to marry him than I have about your reasons for running away. You don't need to explain a thing."

Shanal sat up a bit straighter in her chair. "You really don't like him, do you?"

"Don't like him, don't trust him."

"That's what you tried to talk to me about, back when we announced our engagement, wasn't it?"

He drained his glass. "Another?" he asked, standing up and putting out his empty hand.

"No, thanks, I'm okay. In fact, I think that glass has completely gone to my head. I was too nervous to eat this morning and—"

"I'll go warm up dinner. Mac left us a chicken casserole in the refrigerator. We'll have to cook our own meals from tomorrow."

He went inside before Shanal could realize he'd completely avoided answering her question. But he hadn't counted on her dogged determination to see things to an end. He should have known better. It was what made her a good research scientist, but not necessarily good company right now.

"What was it that you *didn't* say to me at the time, Raif? Why do you dislike him so much?"

"It doesn't matter now."

"I'd like to know."

He set the microwave to reheat and popped the covered casserole dish inside before straightening to face her.

"He killed Laurel," he said simply.

Four

"Raif, that's not true! You know he was cleared of any responsibility in that accident," Shanal cried in response, her smooth brow creasing in disbelief.

"I figured you'd say that. That's why I didn't want to say it to you then, or now."

He turned away and hunted out cutlery and place mats for their meal, then walked past her to set the table.

"You still cold?" he asked, reaching for the switch to turn on the gas heater.

"I'm fine. What do you mean, you figured I'd say that?"

She had a bit more color in her cheeks right now than she'd had all day. Obviously she thrived on conflict and argument more than he'd realized.

"You were engaged to the man. Obviously you'd take his side. And let's face it—we've always been at loggerheads with one another, haven't we? You're hardly likely to believe what I say."

Raif crossed his arms in front of him and stood with his feet planted shoulder-width apart, daring her to contradict his last statement. As he watched her, she lost that air of bravado that had driven her to confront him just now. Her shoulders sagged and she seemed to shrink inside herself.

"I'm sorry you feel that way," she said softly, before lifting her eyes to meet his again. "And yet, despite your opinion of me and my choices, you were the only one who came to help me today."

How did he tell her that he hadn't done it for her as much as he'd done it to defy Burton? Hell, hadn't Raif vowed after Laurel's death that he'd do whatever it took to prevent Burton from hurting another woman, especially one he—?

Raif slammed the door on that thought before it could take wing, and busied himself with finding condiments to put on the table, and throwing the packaged salad he found in the refrigerator into a bowl.

Without actually saying in so many words that he believed the other man was a murderer, he'd tried his hardest to convince Shanal to question her reasons for marrying him. But she'd been adamant. Right up until that crucial moment this morning.

"Raif?" Shanal's voice gently prodded him to respond.

"You were upset and wanted to get away. I was there and I had the means to help you—what else could I have done? I wasn't going to just stand aside and let you be turned into a freak show."

"No, I guess that's bound to come when I return home again."

"It doesn't have to. You can make a statement to the

media and request privacy." He issued a bitter laugh. "Or you could not go home at all."

She shook her head. "It's not quite that simple."

"It can be, if you want it to be."

She averted her gaze, but not before he saw raw grief reflected in her eyes. There was more to this than she was letting on, he just knew it. But how to get it out of her? That was the question.

"Anyway," he continued, "I'm not in a hurry to head back, are you?"

A shudder racked her body. "No."

"Then let's not borrow trouble."

The microwave pinged and Raif retrieved the casserole and put it on the table.

"Come on. Take a seat and have some food."

He lifted the lid of the dish and the delicate aroma of apricot chicken filled the air. Raif ladled a generous portion onto a plate and put it in front of her.

"Help yourself to salad," he instructed, before serving himself.

They ate in silence, Shanal putting away more food than he thought she would, given the circumstances and how tightly she was wound. Halfway through the meal he retrieved their wineglasses and poured them each another serving.

"Trying to help me drown my sorrows?" she asked with a humorless smile.

"Are you sad?" he returned pointedly.

She held his gaze, her determined chin lifting a little, as if in defiance. "Not sad, exactly."

And then her eyes grew shuttered again. She gathered up her plate and cutlery.

"Leave that," Raif instructed. "I'll take care of it."

"I'm not a fragile ornament about to shatter apart,"

Shanal protested as he took the things from her and stacked them in the dishwasher.

"Go, get an early night, and then maybe you'll look less like one," he said firmly, even a little harshly.

There was a flash of hurt in her eyes, which made him realize he'd gone too far. But then he saw her spine stiffen, and a bit of the fire she'd shown earlier returned.

"Fine, then. Since you put it so nicely. I'll go to bed. Did you have a preference as to which room you want to use?"

"I put the bag of clothes in the end room for you. It's the biggest."

"But won't you need clothes now, too?"

"We can stop somewhere along the river and I'll get a few extra things. But I don't need anything else for tonight."

He slept in the nude, always, no matter the weather. Just because he'd rescued a runaway bride wouldn't change that, no matter how her cheeks suddenly flamed with color as she also came to the realization he'd be sleeping naked.

"G-good night, then, Raif."

She turned to go. He put out a hand to stop her, catching her slender fingers in his own. He felt her tremble at his touch, and silently cursed himself for being a boorish idiot.

"I'm sorry I was rude to you."

"No, you weren't," she protested.

"Yes, I was. And I apologize. I shouldn't have taken my frustration out on you. You've had a tough day and it's not you I'm mad at."

To his surprise, Shanal went up on tiptoes and lightly kissed his lips. "Thank you," she whispered.

She pulled her fingers free of his hold and went down

the passage to the bedrooms. He remained rooted to the spot until she closed her door. Half his life he'd waited for that kiss. Fifteen long and often painful years filled with the crazy adolescent yearnings of a first crush. As he grew older and more in control of his emotions, there had even been the occasional dream fantasy that always left him wondering whether they'd be as good together as he'd always imagined. This was the first faint taste he'd gotten in real life of what he'd imagined in such feverish detail.

Her touch had been as delicate as a butterfly's, yet he still felt the imprint on his lips. Still felt the surge of fire through his veins at her closeness. Still wanted her with an ache that put his teenage self to shame. This was going to be one hell of a week; he knew it right down to his bones. Just as he knew that the word *good* couldn't come anywhere near to describing what they'd be like together, should it come to that. In fact, even *incendiary* didn't come close.

In an effort to distract himself, Raif continued to tidy their things away, then poured himself another glass of wine. Maybe the alcohol would dull the allure of imagining Shanal asleep, in something of his, just down the hall. She was a tiny thing and would swim in his stuff. He groaned. This wasn't helping. Even so, the picture of her dainty figure swamped in one of his T-shirts wouldn't budge from his mind.

He went out onto the rear deck and into the cool night air. He stared, unseeing, into the ribbon of river, barely noticeable beyond the lights of the boat, as a cloudy sky obscured all possible star and moonlight. Had he done the right thing in agreeing to come along on this ride with Shanal? Probably not, he had to admit. He'd thought he had this unrelenting attraction he bore for her under control, and yet tonight all that restraint had melted under the merest touch of her lips.

It wasn't as if she'd been the only woman to occupy his mind through these past years. In fact, the reverse was more accurate. He'd had plenty of other relationships, even loved one woman enough to consider asking her to be his wife. But something had always held him back. His reluctance to commit to Laurel had seen her finding solace in Burton Roger's willing arms. And in the end, her life had been snatched away by one careless act.

Careless? Or deliberate? Only one man knew for certain—possibly two, as they'd had a guide on that trip. All Raif knew for certain was that there'd been three people alive at the top of the waterfall that day, and one hadn't survived. It was supposed to have been a controlled descent, but somehow Laurel's rope had failed and she'd fallen horribly before drowning in the water hole at the base of the falls.

A faulty knot, Burton had said, laying the blame fully on Laurel for tampering with a rope he'd already set. And that had been the coroner's finding, too. But once Raif had pared away his grief and studied the incident, he'd felt there was more behind the death of his ex-girlfriend than anyone admitted. Burton had never been what Raif could have called a close friend, but after that incident there was no way Raif had been able to stand being in the same airspace as the guy. He didn't like him and he certainly didn't trust him.

Which brought him full circle back to Shanal. Another woman who needed protection from Burton. Raif would stand by her and keep her safe for as long as she would let him, the way he wished he'd been there to protect Laurel on the trip that day.

* * *

Raif was locked in a nightmare. One where he hovered between the top of the waterfall and the water hole beneath. He saw the terror and panic on her face as Laurel plummeted past him, bouncing off the rocks before hitting the water with a splash and sliding beneath the surface. She was visible through the crystal clear water, and he could see her hair floating out from under the edges of her helmet. He dived into the pool, but no matter how hard he swam, he still couldn't reach her. And still her screams echoed, over and over, "No! No!"

He woke with a jolt, his heart racing and a cold sheen of sweat drenching his body. His chest burned with the breath he still held and he forced himself to let it go, and to try and release the horror of the nightmare.

"No!"

It took him a moment or two to realize he was actually hearing a woman's cry—apparently that part of the dream had been real rather than a figment of his tortured mind. He moved from the bed, reaching for his jeans and skimming them up his bare legs. It took only seconds to swing his door open and follow the passageway to Shanal's room. As he entered he could see her twisted in the sheets, her movements jerky and confined by the cocoon of bedcovers wrapped around her. She moaned in protest and he quickly moved to her side.

"Shanal, wake up, it's just a dream."

Her head thrashed from side to side and he spoke again, more firmly this time, his words a command rather than a suggestion.

In the filtered moonlight from outside he saw her eyelids flicker and open. She stared at him in surprise, her cheeks wet with tears.

"It's okay, you're all right," he assured her.

"I couldn't get away this time," she said in a shaky voice. "He wouldn't let me go."

Raif tugged at the covers that surrounded her. "You probably dreamed that because you've got yourself all caught up in the bedsheets. Here, let me get you free again."

Shanal pushed herself to a sitting position the moment she was free. Her hand shook as she raked it through her hair. "God, that was awful. It felt so real."

"Dreams can be like that," Raif answered, sitting on the bed beside her. His own nightmare continued to leave tendrils of horror clinging to the corners of his mind. "Want to talk about it?"

"I… He… No, not really," she said, wrapping her arms around her torso and giving a little shiver. "Thank you for waking me."

"No problem. I'll leave you to get back to sleep."

He was at the door before she spoke.

"Raif?"

There was a slight wobble to her voice.

"Uh-huh?"

"I know this is probably inappropriate…" Her voice trailed off.

"What is it?"

"Could you stay here with me tonight? I really don't want to be alone."

Stay here? Was she crazy? Hell, was he? He sighed softly in the semidark. Obviously he was.

"Sure."

He waited until she'd settled back down under her covers, and then lay on top of them beside her.

"Thank you. I feel ridiculous, but there's a part of me that's expecting Burton to come through that door any second."

"Not going to happen. He doesn't even know where we are."

"That's good," she answered, her breath a tiny puff of warmth against his bare shoulder. "Um, won't you be cold on top of the covers like that?"

Hardly likely, he thought, given the amount of blood pumping through his system. Did the woman have no idea how alluring she was with her hair all tumbled and dressed only in a thin T-shirt—*his* T-shirt—that did next to nothing to hide the fullness of her breasts or the shape of her nipples through the well-washed cotton?

"I'll be fine. G'night."

He determinedly closed his eyes, even though he could still feel her looking at him, and forced his breathing into a slow and steady rhythm. It didn't take long before he heard her breathing fall into the same deep pattern. He opened his eyes and turned his head on the pillow so he could watch her as she slept.

Her black hair was an inky shadow across her white pillowcase, her eyelashes dark crescents sweeping her face. His gut clenched. Was it possible she was even more attractive asleep? Maybe it was because she seemed softer like this, more approachable. Touchable. He curled his hands into fists, determined not to reach out and touch that silky swathe of hair, or to trace the fine shadow of her cheekbones.

He closed his eyes again. It was going to be a long, long night.

Five

Shanal woke with a deep feeling of contentment and an awareness that she was safe, secure and deliciously warm. Outside she could hear the soft patter of rain. A pair of strong arms, lightly dusted with dark hair, encircled her and she was snuggled up against a very strong, very warm and very bare chest.

A powerful ripple of pure feminine delight spread through her body. Even from between the sheets, she could feel the hard evidence of his arousal. Instinctively she flexed against his hardness, before she realized what she was doing, and with whom.

She pulled away slightly and looked up at Raif's face. Blue eyes, languid with slumber, looked back at her.

"Good morning," she said shyly.

She felt a pang of remorse for moving and waking him when he untangled his arms from around her. Raif sat up and rubbed at his face.

"Good morning to you, too. Did you sleep all right?"

"Like a baby, thank you."

"Good."

He was off the bed and heading for the door before she could protest. But then, what would she say? Would she beg him to stay and hold her again? She buried her face in her pillow. What kind of message was that to send anyone, anyway? Yesterday she'd been ready to marry another man and today she wanted *Raif* to stay and tangle the sheets some more with her? What was she thinking?

Shanal forced herself from the bed and quickly made it before heading to the bathroom. There, she had a hot shower and dressed again in Cathleen's jeans and T-shirt, topping it off with a thick sweater of Raif's she'd found in the bag he'd left in her room. The sweater was far too big for her, of course, reaching to the top of her thighs. She rolled up the sleeves and considered her image in the bathroom mirror. Not too ridiculous, but then again she wasn't here for a fashion show, was she? No, she was supposed to be getting her head straight and figuring out how on earth she was going to solve her family's financial woes, and what she would do if she had no job.

It was ridiculous to think that Burton would still let her keep her position as head of viticulture research and development at the lab. A man like him didn't take kindly to public humiliation. Although, having seen him work the media on more than one occasion, Shanal figured he'd have spun something suitable to ensure he didn't lose face. But spinning the situation undoubtedly meant blaming someone—and that someone would have to be her. So no, she wouldn't have a job anymore.

She loved her work with a passion that didn't extend

to any other part of her life. It was her everything. While she'd always hoped to find love of the kind her parents shared, and which she'd watched bloom between Ethan and Isobel, in the absence of it she'd always been happy to focus solely on her research. While it didn't bring physical reward, it did emotional rewards of a sort, not to mention the recognition and accolades that came along with a job well done.

But if she didn't have her job, she'd have to look for work elsewhere. That could mean leaving Adelaide, leaving her parents. The thought of doing so as her father's illness progressed sent a chill through her. With no extended family in Australia, they were all each other had. She had to hope that Burton would be charitable about her reneging on their agreement to marry, and refrain from blacklisting her with other Australian facilities, even if he didn't allow her to keep her job at Burton International.

A knock on her bathroom door jolted her from her thoughts.

"You okay in there?"

Raif, checking up on her again. What did he think she was going to do? Drown herself in the plug hole? She reached for the door and opened it.

"I'm fine, thanks. Hungry, though. Shall I put our breakfast together?"

"If you'd like. I can cast off and we can start heading upriver while you get it ready."

"Sure," she agreed, pleased to have something to do. Anything, really, to take her mind off the confusion of her thoughts.

In the kitchen, Shanal rummaged through the refrigerator and the pantry.

"How does French toast and bacon sound?" she called to Raif, who manned the helm.

"Better than cereal, that's for sure," he said with a smile that all but took her breath away.

She stood there like an idiot, captured by his male beauty for far longer than was acceptable for people who were merely acquaintances—even if they had shared a bed last night. Shanal forced herself to the business at hand. What was it again? Breakfast. That's right. She flicked a glance back Raif's way. His focus was wholly on the river ahead, which was just as it should be, she told herself sternly.

So what if she had felt a tingle run from head to foot when he'd smiled at her? It didn't mean anything. He was a good-looking guy, and was well aware of his charms—nor was he afraid to use them to his advantage. She'd seen the evidence of that at many a Masters family gathering, when Raif had brought one girl after another. The only girlfriend of his that she'd seen more than once had been Laurel. And, Shanal realized, since the other woman's death, Raif had either been scarce at family do's or had come alone.

Shanal put a pan on the stove to heat for the bacon, and then broke eggs in a shallow bowl and whipped them with a little milk, nutmeg and cinnamon, adding a tiny dash of vanilla extract to the mixture. The cabin soon filled with the scent of frying bacon, and by the time she popped the strips onto a plate in the oven to keep, and added the egg-mixture-soaked bread slices to the pan, her stomach had begun to growl.

"Smells good," Raif commented from his vantage point.

"It's about the only thing I know how to cook well," Shanal said with a laugh. "So I do hope it tastes okay."

"How is that?" Raif asked, turning in his chair to look at her.

"How is what?"

"That you can only cook one thing."

Shanal had the grace to look a bit ashamed. "Even after I left home my mum still cooked for three every night. Before I moved back in with them, she would put meals in her freezer for me and I'd gather them up, a load at a time, when I came over to visit. So I never really had to think about cooking when I got home from work."

Raif laughed out loud and she felt that tingle all over again. Even when he was serious, the man was gorgeous, but laughing? Well, it made something deep inside her clench tight. To avoid examining that odd sensation any further, Shanal quickly turned the bread, then set the table.

"Did you want coffee or tea with breakfast?" she asked, realizing that for all she'd known him half his life, she knew very little about him.

But she wanted to.

Her breath caught on a gasp as she burned herself on the side of the frying pan. Where on earth had that thought come from?

And why now?

"Coffee, please," Raif responded, blissfully unaware of the turmoil she was going through.

"Coming right up."

Ignoring the sting of the burn, she quickly set the coffeemaker to go and added the next batch of bread to the frying pan. In no time the pieces were golden and she plated them up. But with her thoughts still in a whirl, she realized that she wasn't so hungry anymore.

"Breakfast is ready," she said.

"Great, just give me a minute to pull in over there."

He gestured to a small indentation in the riverbank, then nosed the boat in and cut the engine.

"Don't we need to tie off?" Shanal asked.

"We should be okay here while we eat, since we're out of the current. If there's a problem I'll just start her up again."

Shanal poured their coffee and took the mugs to the table. As she did so, Raif's eyes suddenly narrowed.

"Is that a burn?" he asked, grabbing her hand and turning it so he could inspect the redness more closely.

Shanal tried to tug free. "It's nothing."

"It doesn't look like nothing to me. You need to run some cold water over that."

"Seriously, Raif, it's nothing."

He ignored her and led her to the kitchen sink, where he held her hand under the cold tap. The entire time, she was aware of his closeness, of the latent power in his male body, of the gentleness in his touch as he cradled her hand in his. The water might have been cold, but she felt anything but. In fact, heat simmered inside her in a way she'd never experienced before. Heat... and something else.

"How's it feeling now?" Raif asked.

"Fine."

Her voice sounded husky. Embarrassed by her reaction to him, she pulled her hand free and reached for a towel.

"Here, let me." Raif took it from her before she could protest and gently patted her skin dry. "I saw some aloe gel in here before... Ah, here it is," he said, as he poked through a small first-aid box she hadn't noticed on top of the refrigerator.

Raif squeezed a small amount on her hand, his touch light as a feather as he smoothed it over the burn.

"You should be good as new in no time. Any more pain?"

She shook her head. "Thanks, it's good now. Seems I'm always finding reasons to thank you lately," she said, feeling ridiculously shy all of a sudden.

She stepped away from him and reached for the oven door.

"Let me. You go sit down."

"I'm not helpless, you know," she muttered in frustration.

"I know. Tell you what. You can wait on me for the whole rest of the trip. How's that?"

She laughed, her irritation dissolving just as quickly as it had arisen, which was what he'd obviously intended all along. "Fine, I'll do that. But you might be sorry."

"Oh, yeah, that's right. You don't cook. Well, let's see about teaching you, hmm?"

He put their plates on the table and sat down with her.

"This is good," he said, after tasting the toast. "There's something different about it."

"Could be the vanilla essence," she said, accepting his compliment with a buzz of satisfaction.

"Interesting addition."

"It's something my mum does. I learned it from her."

"But not anything else?" he questioned.

"No, not anything else. What about you? Do you cook?"

"Mum made me learn before I went to uni. It was pretty useful when it came to impressing the girls, so I expanded my repertoire pretty quickly."

She rolled her eyes. "Yes, I would have expected that of you."

He shot her a cheeky smile and applied himself to the rest of his breakfast. When they'd finished, he suggested that he get the boat back en route upriver and leave her to guide it while he tidied up.

For the next few hours they lazily cruised along the Murray, taking turns at the helm and admiring the riverbanks as they went along. It was incredibly peaceful, with the exception of the occasional speedboat that went whizzing past, often with a wetsuit-clad wakeboarder hanging off a rope on the back even on a cold day like today.

It was past midday when they reached a small town. The rain had stopped a couple hours earlier and Shanal had been sitting out on the front deck, admiring the ocher-colored cliffs that rose from the river.

"What do you say about a walk?" Raif called to her through the open cabin door.

Shanal started to say yes, but then a memory from the bad dream she'd had last night tickled the back of her mind. She could still recall the all-encompassing fear she'd felt in the dream when Burton had forced her to remain at the altar. She knew it was ridiculous, that her ex-fiancé couldn't possibly have tracked her down yet—and even if he did, he was hardly the violent type—but nevertheless she shook her head. "I'm happy to stay on the boat. But you go on if you want to."

"He's not going to find you here, Shanal. And even if he does, you don't have to go with him."

She closed her eyes and counted slowly to ten. How was it that Raif could read her so easily?

"Okay, I'd like to take a walk with you."

They moored near a ferry landing and then followed the road up the hill and around a sharp bend. It was good to get out of the boat and really stretch her legs, she found, and she enjoyed the view once they made it to the lookout. From there they had a great panorama of the river. Beneath them the ferry plied back and forth, and other houseboats were moored near the terminal on the other side.

"Our boat looks tiny from up here, doesn't it?" she commented.

"It does. I always think a view like this helps remind me to keep things in perspective. When we're on the boat, that's pretty much all we see—aside from the river around us, obviously. Sometimes you just need a bit of distance to rebalance your perceptions. There's so much else that's out there. It makes what we are, what we're going through, seem insignificant sometimes."

"I guess," she agreed, but held the safety railing in front of her in a viselike grip. She wished her problems could fade away into insignificance with just a little distance, but she'd have to return to face them sooner or later. "So, where are we heading from here?"

Raif pointed upriver. "I thought we could keep motoring up toward Swan Reach. Or maybe stop near Big Bend for the night and get to Swan Reach in the morning."

She nodded in agreement and they started the walk back to the boat. As they strolled together, Shanal mulled his words over in her mind. Perspective. That's what he was giving her here by taking her away like this. Time to make her problems seem less insurmountable than they'd begun to be. A tightness invaded her chest as she thought of what might lay ahead. So far, for her at least, the concept of perspective wasn't working all that well. Right now, avoidance was her preference.

She staggered a little as Raif gave her a playful shove.

"You're thinking too hard—I can see smoke pouring from your ears. Come on, I'll race you back to the boat. Last one there makes lunch!"

Her mind latched onto the challenge. With his long legs and strength she had no doubt that he'd beat her, so she took advantage of the fact he was still talking, and started to run.

"You're on!" she shouted over one shoulder.

Rapid heavy footsteps gained steadily from behind, making her squeal.

"I never took you for a cheat," Raif goaded her, from far too close.

"You have to take the advantage where you can!" she laughed, and pushed herself just that little bit harder.

She was out of condition. With helping at home and all the palaver in the lead up to the wedding, combined with her heavy workload, she'd struggled to find time to even do so much as go for a walk each day. She couldn't remember the last time she'd spent any time at the gym. A stitch began to develop in her side but she was nothing if not determined. She would win this race.

Shanal had one foot on the gangplank to the boat, then another, and was about to turn and relish her success when a pair of strong arms wrapped around her and lifted her clean off her feet. She squealed again, this time in surprise, as Raif spun her a full 180 degrees.

"I win!" he crowed as he set foot on the deck and slowly lowered her down, laughing in the face of her frustration.

"And you say *I* cheated?" Shanal said through gasps of air, turning to him in disgust.

"Hey, you forget. I've seen how you can run," he teased, obviously alluding to her bolt from the church yesterday. "I had to use every advantage I had. Besides, I like to win."

"That's not fair," she protested. Was it only a day ago? It felt like forever. Or did she just wish it was?

"All's fair in love and war." He smiled back cheekily.

"You may live to regret that statement," she warned. "Remember, I can't cook."

Raif shrugged. "I also like to live dangerously, don't you?"

She looked at him and felt a tug that pulled from her core. It had nothing to do with her labored breathing and everything to do with the fact that he still had her in the circle of his arms. Her heart was already pumping hard, her senses heightened, and all she could think of was how snugly she fit against him, how close his lips were to hers. How, if she just flexed her hips a little, she'd be nestled in the cradle of his pelvis.

But did she dare?

She did.

Shanal lifted her hands to his head and tugged it down toward her. "I haven't had much cause to live dangerously so far, but I'm willing to give it a try."

And then she kissed him.

Six

She felt the shock roll through his body as her lips touched his. He was unresponsive for a second, then two. She began to wonder if she'd been foolish to do this, to act on the impulse that had overridden her usually careful and considered way of approaching things.

But then his lips began to move over hers, and his arms tightened, pulling her even closer against his body, against his solid strength. Her fingers furrowed through his short dark hair, holding him in place. Not wanting to let him go for a second, because if she did, she'd have to face the questions that would no doubt be in his eyes. Questions she didn't know the answer to herself.

All she knew was that she suddenly realized just how deeply she longed for this. For this man, for his kiss. She slid her tongue softly along his lower lip, felt the shudder that racked his body, felt him harden against her.

This was how it was meant to be between a man and

a woman. Need, desire, want. Not a cold clinical agreement. Not the feeling of being a possession, to be shaped and molded to someone else's taste. Just the need to possess and be possessed in return. She moaned as Raif's tongue touched hers, as a flame of heat speared through her body. She pressed against him, aching for him to fill that emptiness that echoed inside her. Desperate for him to ease the pounding demand that throbbed through her veins.

His hands slid under the sweater she was wearing—his sweater—and the heat of his touch burned through the thin T-shirt that acted as a barrier between his skin and hers. She wanted more. She wanted Raif. Her fingers clenched in his hair and she kissed him more fiercely, her tongue now dueling with his. Advance, retreat, advance again. The taste of him was intoxicating, another sensation to fill her mind and overwhelm her senses.

She felt her nipples tighten into aching buds, and she pressed against him, the movement sending tiny shafts of pleasure to rocket through her body. She'd never felt anything quite like this before. This level of total abandonment, this depth of need.

The sound of the ferry horn echoed across the water—a stark and sudden reminder of where they were, of what they were doing. Shanal let her hands drop to Raif's shoulders as she pulled back. Her entire body thrummed with energy and anticipation, but as she came back to awareness of her surroundings once more, the strength leached from her body, leaving her feeling empty, limp.

"I—" she started.

Raif pressed a short and all-too-sweet kiss to her lips. "Don't say a word. It's okay. To the winner, the spoils, right?"

He bent and lifted the gangplank, stowing it away before he released the ropes that secured the boat to the pier, then he went inside, shrugging off his jacket as he went.

How could he be so nonchalant? As if what they'd just done had meant nothing to him at all? Shanal spun around and gripped the rail that surrounded the deck, desperate to ground herself on something, anything that had substance. Anything that wasn't the emptiness that roared to fill the giant hollow cavern swelling deep inside.

Unexpected tears burned in her eyes and she blinked them back fiercely. What on earth had come over her? She was a rational woman. Not one prone to obeying instinct. Not one who literally flung herself at a man and kissed him until every logical part of her brain was burned into an oblivion of physical awareness.

He'd talked about perspective when they were up on the bluff. She'd never needed it more than she did right now. This was the time for rational thought—for her usual careful deliberation. And yet her body continued to make its demands felt, insisting that she do what felt right without a thought to the consequences. She fought for the equanimity that was her signature in every single thing she did, until every beat of her heart, every breath she took, returned her to a state of lucidity once more. Then and only then would she be ready to face the man inside. At least she hoped she would.

Raif went through the motions, sending the boat back upriver, but he couldn't take his eyes off the woman in front of him. A sheet of glass was all that separated, but it may as well have been a five-foot-thick wall of lead for all the good it did him. Shanal had taken him by surprise, kissing him like that. He should have been a gentleman, should have stepped back right away. Should even have let her win their stupid race instead of grabbing her into his arms as he had. But then he'd always lived life on the wild side—always relished provocation, stimulation. And boy, was he ever stimulated right now.

The fact that he hadn't simply dragged her through to the nearest bedroom and acted on the incredible conflagration that had ignited between them was a testament to his upbringing. His mother would have been proud. Well, except for the kiss, maybe. That, she probably wouldn't have approved of, especially not when the situation between Shanal and Burton was still so murky. Sure, Shanal had removed her ring and run away from their wedding, but Raif had the sense that somehow she was still intrinsically linked to the other man. Whatever was between her and Burton, it wasn't over yet. And Raif didn't like it. Not one bit.

He studied Shanal as she stood on the front deck, staring into the water as if she could somehow find the answer to the meaning of life out there. He wished it was that simple. He'd done his fair share of empty gazing, but all it had taught him was that most often the answers you sought lay within a person, not outside. And sometimes those answers weren't exactly what you wanted to see, either.

"Hey," he called through the door. "You still owe me lunch, remember."

Maybe if he could goad her, as he always had in the past, she'd fire back to life again. He counted several beats before he saw her relinquish the stranglehold she had on the railing and straighten her shoulders once more. She came inside the main cabin, wearing that same fragile, shell-shocked look she'd had yesterday when he'd rescued her in the park. It hit him hard in the gut. He'd put that look on her face by letting their kiss become more than it should have.

"Think you're up to making a sandwich and a pot of coffee?" he prodded.

A faint flare of color brushed her cheeks and a tiny spark of life came back into her pale green eyes.

"I believe I can do that without giving either of us food poisoning," she answered, with her cute little nose up in the air and a haughty expression on her face.

He couldn't help it; he had to smile. It only served to make a frown pull between those perfectly arched brows of hers.

"Life's not a joke, you know," she said in her Miss Prim voice that he already knew so very well.

"No one said it had to be all hard work, either."

He transferred his attention back to the river, but even so he could feel her staring at him. Eventually she gave a small sniff and a few seconds later he heard her rummaging around in the kitchen. Not long after that, a small hand carrying a plate bearing a sandwich appeared in his peripheral vision.

"Thanks," he said, taking it from her. He let his eyes drift over her face, checking to see if the strain of earlier had gone. A sense of relief filled him as she looked back at him steadily. "You okay now?"

She nodded and shifted her attention outside. "I'm not in the habit of kissing just anyone."

"I know," he confirmed.

He was childishly tempted to ask how the kiss they'd shared compared to Burton's, but then pushed the thought from his mind. He didn't want to think of Burton anywhere near Shanal. Not now, not ever.

"It won't happen again," she continued.

"If you say so," he conceded.

"I mean it, Raif. It can't happen again."

There was a thread of panic in Shanal's voice that gave him pause. What had her so scared?

"Shanal, you're safe with me. I'm not going to make you do anything you don't want to do, I promise. But remember, we only get to live this life once. I don't know about you, but I already have enough regrets on my conscience. I don't plan to live the rest of my days with any more."

He had a gutful of regret when it came to Laurel. He'd told her he had concerns about her still being too much of a novice to tackle that waterfall trip. Telling her had been part of what had led to the argument that had eventually seen them break up. He'd never have believed that it would ultimately lead to her death. Regret left a bitter echo in his heart. He didn't want to add to that with Shanal.

Outside, it started to drizzle, then rain more heavily, making visibility on the river difficult. Since they weren't on any timetable but their own, Raif decided to moor the boat along the bank, getting muddy and soaked to the skin as he jumped ashore to tie off the lines. He was chilled right down to his bones by the time he came back on board.

"Why don't you look through the DVDs on the shelf under the TV and see if you can find us something to watch this afternoon," he suggested. "I'm going to grab a quick shower and a change of clothes."

By the time he came back to the main cabin, dressed in an old comfy pair of track pants and a sweatshirt Shanal had handed him from the bag of clothes he'd originally packed for her, she had a couple DVDs on the coffee table. He picked one up.

"You like sci-fi?" he asked.

She nodded.

"Huh, I would have picked you for something else."

"Like what?" Shanal sounded irritated. "Chick flicks?"

He gestured to the Jane Austen boxed set on one side of the shelf. "More that kind of thing."

She shrugged. "I like that, too, but I like this better." She suddenly looked insecure. "Don't you like sci-fi? We can choose something else if you'd rather."

"No, it's okay. I'm a huge Sigourney fan."

"Really? I prefer the alien myself. Such a misunderstood bio-form."

He laughed, plucked the DVD case from her hand and selected the first disc of the set to put in the player. To Raif's surprise, he discovered that not only did Shanal love sci-fi movies, but she also had a very bloodthirsty streak. By the time they were onto their second movie in the trilogy he found himself adjusting a few of his preconceptions about her. Sure, she was incredibly intelligent, but she had a fun side that he'd never seen before. As the alien creature took out a few more good men, she laughed and cheered, all tension from earlier now gone.

He found he really liked her laughter. It wasn't something he'd heard a lot of from her, but when it came it was a joyful gurgling sound that made him laugh right along with her. He found himself ridiculously desperate to hear her laugh some more. And when the movie got really tense and it looked as if all hope was lost for the hero, her dainty hand crept into Raif's for comfort. Squeezing tighter and tighter as the tension rose.

They took a break from movie watching to cook dinner together. Raif supervised as Shanal did most of the work. And he basked in her pleasure as the pasta dish came out better than she'd expected. They ate in front of the TV, watching the last movie in the trilogy, and as the credits began to roll on the screen, Raif caught her yawning.

"Why don't you go on to bed? I'll sort things out in here."

"Are you sure? I don't know why I'm so tired. We've hardly done anything today but watch TV. It must be the rain," she said, getting up from the couch.

Raif missed her presence immediately. He'd grown all too comfortable with her small figure perched next to his on the couch.

"Don't knock it. There's nothing else for you to do right now but sleep, if that's what you want to do," he said, getting to his feet.

The words no sooner left his mouth than a picture of the two of them doing something else in a bed, something that had nothing to do with sleep, imprinted on his mind. His body responded immediately, sending curls of arousal to flick around his all-too-willing flesh. As if her thoughts had taken the same direction, Shanal paused and looked at him—her eyes wide, the pupils dilated. Her hair, worn loose today, was slightly curly and disheveled, making her look younger and more approachable than the tightly buttoned-down and sleek appearance she normally favored.

He decided he liked this side of Shanal Peat just a little too much. It would take very little effort on his part to lean forward and brush his lips against hers. Just a small kiss good-night, that's all it would be.

Liar, a voice sneered in the back of his mind.

"Go on," he said, his voice a little rough. "You head off. I'll see you in the morning."

She bade him good-night and went to her room, leaving him standing there like a starstruck idiot watching his first crush walk away. Then again, she *was* his first crush. There was no doubt about it. But to still feel this way? It was ridiculous. They were both adults now—adults with nothing in common. Except for a love of gory sci-fi flicks and possibly much more.

He shook his head and focused on straightening up the cabin before going to bed himself. There'd be none of that "much more," not after the way she'd reacted after their kiss this afternoon. No matter how much he wanted it. No matter how much he ached for it. But even so, Raif went to bed that night with his door open—just in case she had a nightmare again, he assured himself.

Shanal woke the next morning to the sound of the boat motor running. She rubbed her face and stared at the bedside clock, shocked to realize it was nearly 9:00 a.m. She'd slept almost twelve hours, which was unheard of for her. She shot into her bathroom for a brief shower then quickly dressed and joined Raif.

"Sorry I slept in," she said, as he turned to greet her with one of those killer smiles he specialized in.

"No problem. You must have needed it."

She helped herself to some cereal and a cup of coffee and perched on the seat next to him as he steered the boat upriver. As with everything he did, his hands were strong and competent at the wheel. In fact, she'd never seen Raif Masters at a physical disadvantage with anything. Whether it was operating a post-hole borer to erect uprights for new vine trellises or training the canes along the wires, he approached everything with a surety she sometimes envied. In her line of work, developing new strains of vines, outcomes were not always guaranteed and she often found herself hooked up on data and forgetting that what she was actually doing was creating or improving a living thing. Raif's work was hands-on, all the way. Her gaze lingered on his long broad fingers. Those very same fingers that had caressed her back yesterday as they'd kissed.

A shudder ran through her.

"You cold?" Raif asked.

"No, I'm okay," she said, getting up from her seat and taking her bowl to the kitchen.

But she wasn't okay. She felt disturbed. That kiss yesterday had been all too revealing to her. With it, she'd answered unspoken questions that had plagued her for years. As much as she'd tried to pigeonhole Raif as that cheeky schoolboy she'd met half his lifetime ago, she could no longer do that now. He was very much a man. A man she desired. There. She'd admitted it.

She turned the thought around in her mind, over and over, until she felt almost dizzy with it. During all these years of exchanging verbal barbs with Raif, it had become habit, one designed to create a wall between them. But instead it had created an intangible link. A link that yesterday had become more tangible than not.

It had shaken her to her core, but from the way he'd walked away from her without a second glance, clearly he hadn't had anywhere the same kind of reaction. Why would he? He was a man well used to women throwing themselves at him. In fact, he'd probably found her kiss boring.

Still, there'd been nothing boring about the erection that had pressed against her. He'd been aroused, of that there had been no doubt. And yet he'd later acted as if nothing had happened between them. Shanal tried to tell herself it was a relief that he'd responded that way and had backed off the instant she'd hesitated. But she was female enough to feel piqued that he'd brushed the whole incident off as nothing special.

"We'll be at Swan Reach before lunchtime," Raif said over his shoulder. "We can take a walk around and then have lunch at the pub."

"That sounds great," she answered.

It would be good to be away from the cozy confines of the boat. As comfortable as it was, being out and around other people would hopefully provide some relief from this uncomfortable awareness she'd woken with. And even more hopefully, it would steer her mind clear of the completely inappropriate thoughts she was having toward Raif.

After mooring the boat they strolled to the local museum and spent a surprisingly companionable few hours poring over the displays and documented social history of the area.

"I always love to see these little museums, don't you?" she commented as they headed to the pub overlooking the river for lunch.

"It certainly gives you an insight into how tough people had it and how determined they were to carve out a living with what they had. Makes you realize how lucky we are."

"True, but your family, particularly, have worked very hard to be that *lucky*. You lost everything, and now look at you all."

"Giving up doesn't come easily to a Masters, that's for sure."

Because the sun continued to shine, at the pub they chose to sit outside at one of the picnic tables on a cobbled courtyard. The waitress was quick to bring them each a drink and menus. Shanal was completely relaxed and laughing at some comment Raif had made when she felt her neck prickle uncomfortably with awareness. She turned around, catching a glimpse of a tall man leaving the courtyard and going through the large glass doors that led into the main dining area.

"Someone you know?" Raif asked.

"I don't know anyone here," she said, turning back to face him.

But even so, she couldn't quite shake the uncomfortable feeling that told her the man had been watching her. She was oddly relieved when they returned to the boat and cast off again. She took control of the wheel for the next hour or so before Raif suggested they pull in on the riverside again. After tying off, he put some music on the stereo and challenged her to a game of backgammon. She'd never played before, but she was a quick study, soon grasping the strategy behind the game and beating him soundly several times. Several games in, she realized that Raif was spending more time watching her, and studying her expressions as she analyzed the board, than concentrating on the game. Eventually, he threw up his hands and cried uncle when she beat him once again.

"Remind me not to be such an awesome tutor next time," he grumbled good-naturedly as she packed up the counters and board.

"Oh dear, was that a blow to your masculinity?" she teased back with mock sympathy.

"Ha, it'd take more than that to knock me down. Now, if you want to challenge me to an arm wrestling match…?"

She laughed aloud. "I think I'll pass on that. I know where my strengths lie."

"You hungry?"

She looked at the time and realized how long they'd been playing backgammon. "I could eat," she admitted, surprised to find it true, even though it hadn't been all that long since lunch.

But then again, she'd ended up only picking at her lunch after that unsettling feeling she'd had of being watched. It had left a shadow lingering in the back of her mind that even now had a presence. She forced herself to ignore it again.

"Come on then. Time for cooking lesson number two."

Shanal followed Raif to the kitchen, where he selected a series of ingredients from the vegetable crisper in the fridge and extracted a couple packets she couldn't identify. Raif began to chop vegetables with an ease that spoke of much practice.

"Now, the key," he said, chopping swiftly, "to impressing your dinner partner is to deliver food to the table that looks as though you slaved over it all day, when in actual fact it only takes a few minutes to throw together."

"Is that so?" Shanal leaned against the counter and watched him, mesmerized by the movement of his hands and how he managed to keep his fingers clear of the flashing blade. "And you've impressed a lot of dinner partners, I take it?"

"I suppose I've dazzled my share," he replied with false modesty, making her laugh again.

"What are you cooking tonight?"

"Me? I'm just doing the grunt work. You're doing the cooking and it'll be a seafood stir-fry, okay?"

She nodded. "I love seafood."

He winked in return. "Me, too."

He showed her how to prepare the squid and left her to it while he poured them each a glass of wine.

"Life doesn't get any better than this," he commented, before handing her wine to her and raising his glass. "To a good life."

Shanal wiped her hands and took the glass, clinking it against his. "A good life," she repeated, then took a sip.

The words were so simple, so easy to say, but while she had it good here and now, she had some serious decisions to make soon. She couldn't keep running away forever, no matter how much she wanted to. It wouldn't be fair to her parents, after she'd already let them down so badly. Yet Shanal looked up at Raif and realized that she'd happily run away with him forever.

She sighed. This was ridiculous. She couldn't feel that way about someone she'd actively avoided for so long it had become second nature. But then life wasn't simple, was it? She'd never have believed in a million years that her normally astute father would have put all his eggs in one very broken financial basket, either. Or that he'd have done something as stupid as risk a life out of pride. But he had, and his mistakes had left him and her mother so terribly weak—financially, physically and emotionally.

Was that what this was for her? A mistake? By running away from Burton as she'd done, she'd acted very irrationally indeed. But as hard as she tried, she couldn't regret it. And as hard as she tried, she could no longer ignore her attraction to Raif. His good looks were undeniable, but it was the man beneath all that male beauty that drew her like a magnet. That made her dream stupid dreams and hope ridiculous things for the future.

Shanal resolutely turned her mind back to the meal

she was preparing under Raif's excellent and patient tutelage, and tried to ignore the ember of warmth that glowed a little brighter every time their hands brushed, or whenever he accidentally bumped into her as they worked side by side in the small kitchen. She drank a little more liberally of her wine than she would normally, enjoying the delicious lassitude that spread through her veins, and taking pleasure in the moment.

Her life was usually so structured, so detail oriented, that it felt positively sinful to be so relaxed. She'd make the most of it while she could. The meal, when she plated it up, was delicious, and when Raif opened another bottle of wine she didn't object, instead holding her glass to him for a refill. It was a clear night, although cold, and they took a couple throw blankets outside with them to watch the stars as they enjoyed their after-dinner drink.

It felt completely natural to curl up next to Raif on the wicker two-seater sofa on the front deck, and with the cabin lights off behind them, to enjoy the reflection of the moon and stars on the gently rippling river. Soft drifts of classical music filtered on the night air from inside, and when Raif lifted his arm to drape it behind Shanal's shoulders, she didn't object, nor did she pull away.

"Look," he murmured, "a shooting star."

"Probably just space junk," Shanal commented with a tiny spark of her usual levelheadedness.

"Where's your sense of romance?" Raif chided gently. "Go on, make a wish."

She thought about where she was and what she had yet to face. A wish? Why not? It was a simple thing, after all, and who knew what lay around the bend? She closed her eyes and wished with all her heart.

"Did you make one?"

"I did," she replied.

"What was it?"

"Isn't it supposed to mean a wish doesn't come true if you tell someone?"

"Are you telling me you've overcome your scientific nature and become a believer in wishes now?" he retorted, but without a sting in his voice.

She hesitated a moment, then put her glass down on the deck before turning to face him in the darkness. "I wished for you."

Seven

For the first time in his life that he could remember, Raif didn't know what to say. His breath caught in his chest, leaving it tight and aching. Much like another part of his anatomy. The silence stretched out between them.

"To be precise," Shanal eventually said in a small voice, "I wished for you to make love to me."

Every cell in his body urged him to seize the moment and take her up on her wish, but an unwelcome voice of reason whispered in the back of his mind. Why now? Was she looking for rebound sex? They hadn't even touched on her reasons for leaving Burton at the altar, mainly because of Raif's own reticence about hearing them. But whatever those reasons were, did he really want to be her rebound guy?

His hesitation must have communicated itself to Shanal because she suddenly ducked her head and drew away from him.

"I'm sorry. I'm being ridiculous. Probably too much wine. Don't mind me."

She started to get up from the couch, but his arm shot out, his hand clasping hers and pulling her back. He caught her chin between his fingers and lifted her face to his.

"Are you sure, Shanal? Is that what you really want?"

What the hell was he doing, asking her? She'd already said what she wanted and his body was certainly eager and willing to make her wish come true. A little too willing, if the current fit of his jeans was any indicator. He wasn't going to let his hormones take over. If he—if *they*—did this, it would be for the right reasons. And why was he even considering this? Was it to assuage all those pent-up, lustful teenage dreams he'd suffered for so long, or did it have more to do with getting back at Burton Rogers? He thrust the idea of the other man to the recesses of his mind. Burton was not going to intrude on whatever this evening turned out to be. Shanal deserved better than that and hell, so did Raif. He'd wanted her for what seemed like forever and he was more than ready, but she had to be certain. She had to come to him freely, unreservedly, or not at all.

Time crawled to a halt as he waited for her response.

He barely heard her answer when it came, but the softly spoken "yes" was all he needed. He bent his head and caught her lips with his. What he'd planned to be a sensitive and careful caress turned molten as she kissed him back. Her arms snaked around his waist and she pressed her body up against his as if he was a refuge from all the fears she held deep inside. Maybe that's all he was to her right now, but he'd take that, and more.

She was perfection in his arms. Her small frame fitted neatly against his. The softness of her curves melted into him as if the two of them had been carved from one piece. She moaned as he deepened their kiss, as his tongue met hers, as he caressed the roof of her mouth. Her hands found their way under his sweatshirt, tugging at his T-shirt until she touched his flesh.

It was everything he'd ever anticipated and yet not enough at the same time. They were too restricted here, and there was so much he wanted to do with her. So very much. He scooped her into his arms.

"Inside," he growled. "I want to see you. All of you."

"Yes," she whispered in return, her hands reaching for his face and drawing him to her to kiss again.

She was heat and hunger and everything he'd always dreamed she'd be. The kiss they'd shared yesterday had been only a prelude to this moment—the denouement of years of fighting his feelings for her, of subjugating his desire for her. He made their way to his room in the dark, but once there, he laid her down on the bed and reached to switch on the bedside lamps, bathing the room in a warm golden glow. He didn't want to miss seeing a single second of this.

He reached for her, guiding her clothing from her body, exposing her natural beauty to him and relishing the sensation as his palms and fingers caressed her skin and absorbed her heat, letting it mingle with his own. He skimmed his hands up from her tiny waist and over her narrow rib cage, then filled his palms with her breasts before bending down to take her nipple in his mouth. He rolled the peaked flesh with his tongue, pulling softly, feeling a pulse of satisfaction at the moan of pleasure that fell from her swollen lips.

"You are so beautiful," he murmured against her skin.

The words may have been clichéd, but to him, at this

moment, there was nothing better to be said. She *was* beautiful, and right now she was his. He had waited years for this moment and he wasn't about to rush any part of it. He wanted to burn this night into his memory forever. And not just this one night, if he had any say about it. Every night from now on sounded just about perfect.

"You make me feel beautiful," she whispered in return, her voice tinged with wonder. "*You* make me *feel*."

The unspoken message in her words hung in the air between them. He made her feel? What did she mean by that? Had no one ever taken the time to make her feel beautiful, desirable before? Not even the man she had promised to marry? Raif found that hard to believe, but then again, he'd thought there had always been an untouchable air about Shanal. Maybe he needed to revise that thinking. Maybe she carried more of an air of being untouched?

"Shanal? You're not—?"

"A virgin? No. But I don't have a great deal of experience. No one has ever…moved me the way I feel right now," she admitted shyly.

Whoever she'd been with and whatever the circumstances, Raif would make sure that this time, with him, she felt everything that lovemaking could be between two people. She would be as engaged in what they did together as a person could possibly be.

With that in mind, he transferred his attention to her other breast, sucking and pulling gently at her dark brown nipple until it, too, was as taut as its twin. He shifted so he could kiss her lips again, his hands never leaving her breasts, his fingers rolling and tugging at their tips until she began to squirm beneath him.

She kissed him back with a ferocity that made his

blood burn in his veins, scorching him until his entire body was aflame. He'd thought to keep the barrier of his clothing to remind him not to rush things, but found he could no longer wait to feel her body against his, skin on skin, heat on heat, hardness on softness. Her hands were there to help him as he sat up and pulled his sweat-shirt and T-shirt off in one sweep, his skin prickling in tiny goose bumps as her fingertips swept over his torso.

He felt ridiculously clumsy as he fought with the button fly of his jeans and finally shimmied out of the restrictive denim. His briefs, too, came off in haste. He almost groaned in relief as his straining erection was finally free of constraint, but the sense of freedom was short-lived as Shanal's fingers closed around him like a velvet glove.

His eyes slid closed and Raif clenched his jaw with the strain it took not to thrust against her gentle ca-ress, not to give in to the base need that threatened to overwhelm him. Her touch was tentative, exploratory—though she was clearly gaining confidence with each stroke, each featherlight touch. When she reached the aching head of his penis a shudder ran through his body. He opened his eyes and caught the smile of satisfaction on her face.

"You're driving me over the edge," Raif warned, his voice low and tight with need.

"I love that I can do this to you," she answered, her eyes glowing with need. "You're always so confident, so sure of yourself, but like this? In this moment you're vulnerable, and I can't help but wonder at the fact that it's because of me."

Did the woman have no idea of the allure she'd held for him all these years? Clearly, she hadn't the faintest clue that from the first day he'd met her he'd alternated between teenage angst and fighting some crazy hormonal response to her nearness every time they'd been in the same room. She'd always had this effect on him, long before tonight. Hell, even thinking about her had given him a raging hard-on—then and now.

"I'm at your disposal. All yours," he said. "Do what you want with me."

There, he'd handed over the reins to her, to let her act rather than be acted upon. She gestured for him to lie on the bed beside her, and kissed him the moment his head hit the pillow. Her mouth was hot and wet and demanding; her teeth gently abraded his lower lip before she began her exploration of his body.

"I've wondered what you felt like, what you tasted like," she said, positioning herself over him and rising onto her knees.

Her hands were spread like small fans over his chest, her fingertips tracing the shape of his nipples. Raif found himself ultrasensitive to her touch, not to mention the heat of her lower body as she settled over his groin. Shanal leaned down to mimic the movements of her fingers with the tip of her tongue, and he felt her touch all the way to the soles of his feet, his body attuned to her every movement, her every caress.

"Mmm," she murmured, "I like the way you taste."

Her mouth closed over his nipple and she bit gently on the sensitive skin, sending another bolt of sensation plummeting through him. Her long hair slid over him like a drift of silk. He didn't know how much longer he could take this and not lose control, but he reminded himself to stay strong, to let her take the lead the way he'd promised she could.

Somehow he found the strength to hold back, to allow her to continue her voyage of discovery as she followed the contours of his ribs, his abdomen, his belly. But when she began to slide farther down, he knew it was time to take charge again, or it would be all over before it truly began.

Raif flipped her so she lay on her back, her glossy black hair a wave of darkness across the pristine white pillow, her eyes glazed with desire for him. A smile curved those beautiful, sweet lips of hers as she looked up.

"So, I can do to you what you do to me." She said it as a statement, as if she'd discovered some incredible phenomenon.

"And what is that, exactly?" he asked, bending his head to nip at the lushness of her smile.

"Drive you crazy."

"Completely and utterly over the edge."

Even as he spoke, his hands were busy, one supporting most of his weight, the other sliding inexorably down to the apex of her thighs. He felt her heat, her wetness, and groaned.

"You're so ready."

"Then take me," she urged, pressing her mound against the palm of his hand. "Make me feel some more."

"You want me?"

He circled her center with the pad of his thumb, his fingers cupping her moist entrance.

"Yes, oh yes."

Shanal's breath came in short sharp gasps as he increased the pressure of his thumb, incrementally nearing that point of pleasure, taking delight in the uninhibited yearning that spread across her face. He eased one finger inside her, felt her instant response as she clenched tight around him.

"You like that?" he asked, brushing his lips over hers again.

"More, give me more, please," she begged.

Her hands cupped his face and held him to her. Her lips, her tongue, responded to his in feverish delight. He eased a second finger inside her welcoming sheath, and increased the tempo of his thumb, his tongue now mimicking the movement of his fingers as he dipped and dived into the cavern of her mouth in tandem with the center of her core. He felt the moment she tipped over the edge as her body went rigid and strained against him, her fingers now curled tight in his hair, tugging against his scalp as, with a keening cry, she fell into the abyss of orgasm. Her body shook and trembled beneath him and he ached to follow her into that moment of bliss, barely managing to hold himself back. Slowly, gently, he quieted his movements.

After a few moments Shanal moved beneath him. "So that's what everyone raves about? I had no idea. I mean, I've enjoyed sex before but…wow, not like that."

He couldn't help but feel an inordinate amount of pleasure that he should be the one to shatter her past experience into oblivion.

"That's just the beginning," he said. "We've got all night long."

"Thank goodness," she said with a small laugh. "Because I really want to do that again."

"I've created a monster," he groaned theatrically.

"Then I suggest you do something to soothe the beast," Shanal responded, her hands back at his erection. "Because there was something missing in that last effort."

"Missing?"

"Yes, you."

"Well, let's see about correcting that, shall we?"

* * *

Shanal laughed softly, still amazed at the level of response this incredible man had coaxed from her body, and how, instead of leaving her sated, it had left her wanting more. More of him. And the laughter. She'd never laughed in such intimate circumstances with anyone before, yet with Raif everything was okay—natural. She shifted again so she was astride him, and positioned herself over his straining flesh.

"Shanal, wait, we don't have—" Raif started.

But then she lowered herself onto him, taking him into her body, into her heart.

"Shanal," he said again. "We—"

Again his voice cut off as she clenched his length with her inner muscles, the movement sending off ripples of exquisite sensation to spiral through her body. It was as if, having reached that miraculous height he'd brought her to just a little while before, her body now knew exactly what it wanted and exactly how to get it. It was liberating, and he'd done this for her. She moved, rocking and allowing him to withdraw slightly, before plunging down and rocking forward again and again and again, until she lost track of reason and time and could feel only pleasure as it built and built within.

Raif's hands were at her hips, her breasts, everywhere. She felt her body straining toward completion and then it began—that starburst of intense joy, that sense of complete rightness. She looked down, lost in her voyage of discovery, her gaze locked with Raif's. His hips pumped in unison with the movements of her body, his hands now clenched on her hips as he strained upward as if he wanted to lose himself in her forever. And then he hit his peak, his hips jerking, his arms closing around her to pull her down over him, crushing her against his chest as their bodies pulsed in unison.

It felt like eons later that Raif's hands drifted to her back, to caress the length of her spine, to cup her buttocks. Her head rested on his chest, and beneath her ear she could hear his heart still pounding, as hers no doubt did, too. She felt him withdraw from her and made a sound of objection.

"Shanal," Raif said, lifting a hand to brush her hair off her face.

"That was incredible," she sighed against the warmth of his skin, before pressing a kiss right there.

"It was, but sweetheart, we didn't use protection. Are you on the pill?"

"Yes, of course."

She was on a low-dose contraceptive. Anything else created unpleasant side effects for her.

"But you don't have your pills with you."

"True," she acknowledged, and while the scientist in her told her she'd been all kinds of crazy to have sex with Raif unprotected, the woman inside her told her that everything would be fine. "I'll be okay, I'm sure."

"From here on in, we use condoms."

"You brought some with you?" she asked, lifting her head and raising an eyebrow in surprise.

"No, silly." He gave her a gentle slap on her behind. "There are some in the bathroom."

"Then what are we waiting for?" she teased, sliding off him. "They're no good to us in there."

Eight

Shanal eased from the bed as daylight began to trickle through the windows. Her body felt well used and she could barely keep the smile from her face as she made her way to the bathroom. After relieving herself, she studied her body in the mirror. She should look different after the transformative experience she'd shared with Raif last night, and yet she was still the same old Shanal. Short, neat figure—nothing spectacular. And yet in his arms she'd felt like one in a million—a rare prize to be cherished. No one had ever made her feel this way or taken her to such heights before in her life. In fact, she never wanted to even think about making love with anyone other than Raif after last night.

Locked in the band of intimacy they'd created, Shanal had come to realize some truths in the night. The first being an understanding of why she'd always kept Raif at arm's length for the whole time they'd known one another. She'd instinctively sensed, somehow, just how shattering an effect he would have on her.

How would she have met her educational goals if she'd succumbed to him before she'd completed her doctoral degree? Where would she be right now? Having tasted the glory he offered, she had no doubt that he would have clouded her mind so much that she would have been happy to sacrifice the personal goals she'd always used to drive herself. No, their time and place had not been back then, in the past. But it was here and it was most definitely now.

Raif appeared in the doorway behind her, closing the short distance between them and wrapping her in his arms. He rested his chin on top of her head and met her eyes in the mirror.

"You okay?"

"Never better." She smiled.

"No regrets?"

"None."

"Then come back to bed."

She could already feel his arousal pressing against her, and in that short sweet moment she felt her body react in kind. In the mirror she saw her nipples bead into taut points and a flush of warmth spread over her chest. He did this to her—no, she thought, he did this *for* her. She turned in his arms and lifted her face for his kiss.

They were both starving when they eventually woke again. After a leisurely shower together they made breakfast and ate it on the rear deck of the boat, looking out over the river. Shanal felt tired but invigorated at the same time. And for the first time in the past several weeks she felt as if she could tackle all the worries in her life head-on. A solution to her father's problems had to be able to be found, in a way that would preserve his dignity and still allow for both her parents to enjoy the years they had left together—without requiring Shanal to sacrifice her own life.

"Where are we headed to next?" she asked as they cleaned up the kitchen after breakfast.

"We'll get through Lock 1 and stop at Blanchetown if you like. We could do the historical walk around town or go a little ways out and visit the conservation park."

"Both sound good. Let's play it by ear, shall we?"

They continued up the river. Raif gave three long blasts on the boat's air horn to signal the lock attendant as they approached. Shanal watched with interest as a red flashing light on top of the control box let Raif know a chamber was being prepared for them. Once it was filled with water, they were given a green flashing light to proceed. The whole process went incredibly smoothly and before long they'd passed under the Sturt Highway bridge and were tied up at a new mooring.

Shanal and Raif got off the boat and, arms linked and laughing, headed toward town. She hadn't felt this carefree in forever, she thought, or cared less about how well she was groomed. She was dressed today in one of Raif's long-sleeved T-shirts, topped by a voluminous checkered bushman's shirt, which she'd tied in a clumsy knot at the waist of his sister's jeans. No designer fashion underneath a prim white lab coat for her today, and she'd never felt happier.

As they walked under the bridge, a movement caught her eye, drawing it to a familiar BMW parked near the massive struts that supported the structure. Suddenly she understood that odd sensation she'd experienced yesterday back at the pub where they'd stopped for lunch. That sensation of being watched. Somehow, Burton had tracked them down. He must have had his spies out all along the river, on the lookout for them. After all, it wouldn't have been too hard to have found Raif's Jeep parked back at the marina in Mannum, and worked out the rest from there. Finding her location today had simply been a matter of continuing on the route from yesterday. A sick feeling of dread filled Shanal and she tightened her fingers on Raif's arm.

"What—?" he started to say, then stopped as he realized where she was looking.

She felt him stiffen, and didn't object when he broadened his stance and pulled her behind him. Despite knowing he wanted to protect her, she found the nerves in the pit of her stomach knotting as the driver's door of the car opened. For the briefest second she wondered if she was wrong, if she'd mistaken the make and model of car for someone else's, but then the driver unfolded from inside the vehicle.

Tall, with dark blond hair and a slim build, Burton was impeccably polished as usual. She saw his eyebrows rise slightly as he walked toward them and took in her appearance.

"Slumming it, Shanal?" he said silkily. "That's not like you."

"What are you doing here, Burton?" Raif demanded, before she could respond.

"Why, I'm here for my bride, of course."

"She's not your bride and she's not your possession."

"Well, we'll see about that, won't we," Burton replied, with a smile that held all the warmth of a glacier. "Shanal, could we talk? In private please."

Shanal suppressed a shudder at the saccharine tone in his voice. She wanted nothing more than to grab Raif's hand and run away—get on the boat and out on the river and never look back. And she could still do that. She knew without a doubt that if she asked him, that's exactly what Raif would do. But realistically, she knew she couldn't run away forever. She didn't just have herself to consider. The weight of her father's problems returned to lie across her shoulders like a cape of lead.

"You don't have to do anything you don't want to do," Raif said to her as she started to move out from behind him.

"It's okay. I knew I'd have to talk to him sometime. It may as well be now."

Raif hooked one arm around her and pulled her to him, kissing her fiercely before letting her go. "I'll be waiting right here for you."

She lifted one hand to stroke his cheek with her fingertips. "I know," she breathed softly. "That means everything to me."

"How touching," Burton commented. "I suppose you think you're one up on me now, Masters?"

"I'm always up on you, Burton."

Shanal could hear the loathing in Raif's voice as he answered his old nemesis.

"Funny, I don't believe Laurel felt the same way. As I recall, she chose me over you."

"Don't you dare bring her into this." Raif started to move forward, his hands clenched into fists, but stopped when Shanal put a hand on his chest to halt him.

"Don't, Raif. He's just baiting you," she pleaded.

"Don't dare? Or what?" Burton jeered. "You'll take my fiancée from me again? I don't think so. You'll remember that Laurel left you for me. I don't suppose you told many people that, did you? That she was with me because you weren't enough for her anymore. While you secreted Shanal away in your love nest on the water over there, did you share that piece of information with her?

Does she realize that these past few days have probably been little more than a childish tit for tat? You attempting to get back at me for Laurel choosing me over you."

"Laurel would never have been happy with you. Don't kid yourself into believing differently," Raif growled.

"Oh, really. Perhaps it was more accurate that she would never have been happy with you. She saw that you wouldn't, or perhaps more accurately *couldn't*, offer her what she needed, the way I did. The way I'm doing for Shanal now."

"Shanal, are you coming?" Burton changed tack, his voice once again sickly sweet. "Don't let him trick you any longer, darling. I'll forgive you for this episode if you come with me now. Trust me, this was more about his need to poke at me than any real desire for you. I'm prepared to overlook that and forget all about this if you'll come back where you belong."

Shanal threw Raif a silent plea to refute those poisonous words. What he'd suggested, that Raif had taken her away only to get back at Burton, was nothing but spite on the part of a man thwarted in his goals, surely. When Raif said nothing, she had to ask him.

"Revenge, Raif? Seriously? Was that what all this was about?"

He stood stoic and strong, his eyes not budging from Burton, as if he didn't trust the man one inch. "No."

"But you thought of it, didn't you?" she asked, desperate to know the truth.

"Far as I know, a man can't be condemned for his thoughts."

But he could be condemned for his actions. Had everything about these past couple days been a lie? Had their night of loving been no more to him than a means to an end, driven by rivalry with Burton rather than real feelings for her? Shanal didn't want to believe it was true, but Raif said nothing to tell her differently. He seemed more determined to continue the now silent standoff between the men than to assure her he hadn't been using her.

"Shanal, come with me," Burton instructed. "I promise you, if you come now, everything will be as it was before. I have a message for you, too. From your father. He's counting on you."

Shanal almost got whiplash from the speed at which she spun her head to look at him. The threat implied in his words was clearer than anything he'd ever said before.

"What's he talking about?" Raif asked.

"Nothing," Shanal said automatically, so used to keeping her father's shameful secret that she couldn't bring it out into the open now. The time for confidences in Raif was gone. She cast one more look at him, silently begging him to contradict Burton's accusations—to be someone she could trust again. But even if he did, she was still caught between a rock and a hard place. A helpless sense of the inevitable seeped like a dark fog into her mind.

"Remember just how much you have hanging on this," Burton reminded her in an undertone. "Your job, the roof over your parents' heads. And if you think your father's still worried about his reputation, I can only imagine how he'd feel to see yours raked through the muck along with his."

Shanal bit the inside of her mouth to hold back the cry of protest that instinctively rose. The writing was on the wall. If she didn't go back with Burton, she wouldn't have a job or a reputation left. It would be no hardship for him to use his extensive network and power to ensure that she didn't find work again in Australia. Possibly even overseas, as well. Anyway, seeking work overseas was a moot point with her parents needing her so much and her father's illness progressively getting worse. But without the income from her job, how would she be able to take care of her parents?

"I'm losing patience," Burton said with an ugly twist to his mouth. "Figure out what you want, *darling*. You are running out of time."

It was what he left unsaid that drove her to her decision. She knew he wouldn't hesitate to act. To make both hers and her parents' lives hell. There was only one thing left she could do.

"I'm coming, but let me say goodbye to Raif—alone," she added, when Burton made no move to get back into his car.

"Two minutes, no more," he conceded.

The second his car door was closed Raif caught her by her arms. "You don't have to do this," he said urgently.

She looked into his eyes and knew this was the end of what they'd shared together. "Yes, I do. Look, whatever your reasons for helping me, I am grateful at least for the fact you got me away from a situation I wasn't comfortable with."

"What about us?"

"Good question." She dived on his words. "What Burton said about you wanting to hurt him, that was true, wasn't it?"

"I can't lie, Shanal. Not to you. There's bad blood between us and yes, it did cross my mind and give me a certain amount of pleasure to know that spiriting you away would drive him crazy."

She felt Raif's words as if they were tiny cuts across her heart. "Then that's all I needed to know."

"But that's not all," he persisted. "It might have started that way—back in the park, at the very beginning—but it isn't how I feel now. Not about you, Shanal."

"How can I believe you?" she asked desperately, tears filling her eyes and obscuring her vision. "Let's be honest, Raif. For years we've been sparring with one another. We've never seen eye to eye and it's not as if we were ever friends. I'm the fool. I should have questioned your willingness to help me in the first place."

And really, what did it matter whether she believed him or not? Staying with him wasn't an option, even if he truly wanted her to. She had only one choice available to her: she had to go back with Burton. That crushing sense of how inescapable her situation was now consumed her. She pulled away.

"I have to go. He won't wait forever."

"Let him leave then."

"I can't."

She forced herself to turn away from Raif and walk toward the car. Burton got out as she approached and strode around to the passenger side to hold the door open for her.

"Looks like history repeats itself," he taunted. "And yet again, I win the girl."

Nine

Raif watched as the BMW drove away, his body a mass of bunched muscle still tensed in shock. He couldn't believe what had just happened. That Shanal had chosen Burton over him. Burton's parting jeer echoed in his head, and a red film of rage crossed Raif's vision. The man was toxic. He'd twisted the truth of what had happened in the past—surely Shanal had to see that.

So why had she chosen to return to him? There had to be more to it. She was an intelligent woman and she had to see that things didn't add up with Burton. The man always had an agenda, always had to be on top— by fair means or foul.

Even when they'd been at private school together he'd been competitive, but that had been nothing compared to how competitive Burton had become as they'd grown into adulthood. Nothing was sacred anymore. Burton had crossed the bridge between good-natured rivalry

and the out and out need to win at any cost long before they'd finished high school. Raif had felt the rifts
in their camaraderie—for they had never truly been
friends—years ahead of the issue with Laurel.

But none of that meant anything right now, he
thought as he watched the taillights on the BMW flick
once before it turned and disappeared from view. All
that mattered was that the woman who'd blown his mind
and his body into new realms had walked away from
him for good.

Raif strode back to the houseboat. There was nothing
keeping him here now. He needed to get back downriver
and home. As he shoved off and headed back toward
the lock he considered everything that had happened
in the past four days. It had been such a short time and
yet it felt like so much longer.

After passing through the lock and setting his course,
Raif let his mind mull over the final confrontation.
Though he hadn't heard everything they'd said to each
other, there'd been an undercurrent between Shanal and
Burton. He'd felt it as if it was a tangible thing. Their
body language had not been that of lovers, that was for
sure. In fact, when he thought back to the church—to
before that moment when Shanal had dropped her bouquet, given Burton back his ring and headed for the
door—Raif had noticed already the sense of triumph
in Burton's posture. As if Shanal was a prize he'd won,
rather than the woman he loved and wanted to spend
the rest of his life with.

Raif knew Shanal deserved more than that in her
life partner. In fact, he'd always believed she wanted
more than that, too. Even Ethan had said the same after
that botched business when he'd asked Shanal to marry
him, as part of his misguided efforts to avoid admitting

his own feelings about Isobel a couple years back. If Shanal was the kind of woman who was just after what money could bring her, or even if she simply wanted a marriage that brought practical benefits and made logical sense, she'd have accepted Ethan's offer with alacrity, not laughingly but lovingly turned him down. And Ethan was her best friend—someone she always looked at with warmth and affection, even if there was no heated passion between them. There had been no warmth or affection in her expression when Shanal looked at Burton.

Raif thought about the niggle he'd had a day or so ago, suspecting there was way more to this than met the eye. His instincts hadn't let him down before and he had no reason not to trust in them now. And even if he was wrong about Shanal and what she really wanted, he needed to know the truth, for his own sake. If he was right, and he fully expected to be, somehow he'd convince her to walk, hell, *run* away from Burton again. And this time, he'd hold on to her and keep her safe forever.

Traveling back on his own had been harder than Raif had anticipated. First there was the physical evidence of their passionate lovemaking to contend with. Second was the physical memory of expecting her to be by his side when he worked in the kitchen or even here, at the helm of the boat. The houseboat was not large and yet it felt echoingly empty without Shanal there beside him. He couldn't get away from it fast enough. What had taken them a leisurely few days to travel upriver, he accomplished in half the time, heading back down.

Mac was at the marina to greet him.

"Everything handle okay?" the older man said.

"Like a breeze," Raif replied, tossing him the rope to tie off.

"Where's your little lady?"

"Gone home with her fiancé," he answered, unable to keep the bitterness from his voice.

"Her what?"

"Yeah, Burton Rogers. You remember him?"

"Remember him, sure. Ever want to see him again? No. I couldn't understand it when Laurel left you for him. I thought I'd raised her to have better judgment than that. But I think she was swayed more by what he could offer her than by who he was. I've always like to think that if she'd lived, she'd have eventually figured him out and left him."

Raif just grunted in response. After all, what could he say? That he'd stood by and not fought back when she'd given him an ultimatum about marriage or breaking up? He hadn't been ready for that commitment. But he certainly hadn't been ready to lose her altogether, either. And the thought that his choice had driven her into Burton's arms and from there to her death… No, he wouldn't let himself think about that.

"What happened?" Mac asked.

Raif gave him a brief rundown once he was off the boat.

"And you let her go?" There was censure in the older man's voice.

Raif wanted to vehemently deny it, but he couldn't. "She was never mine to hold on to."

Mac stared out at the slow-moving river. "You know, I never held with that saying about letting love go free. I've always thought that if you really want something, you gotta hunt it down and fight to keep it."

"My thoughts exactly," Raif concurred, picking up his bag. "And that's just what I'm going to do."

"That's my boy." Mac slapped him approvingly on the shoulder.

Raif drove back to his home in the Adelaide Hills in heavy rain, which meant he had to keep his concentration very firmly on the road ahead and not on his plans to get back Shanal, where he wanted it to be. But the minute he walked through his front door he was reminded of the last time he'd returned home, and who he'd had with him.

There was a note from his cleaner on the hall table:

I have hung the wedding dress that was on the floor in the guest room en suite on a hanger in the guest room wardrobe. Please inform me if you need the garment sent to the dry cleaner.
—H.

Raif cracked a wry smile. It would have been worth it to see the expression on his cranky cleaner's face when she came across that little surprise. He went to the spare room to see the dress in question.

It hung in all its subdued glittering splendor on the rail, the layers of froth at the bottom almost filling the generous space of the wardrobe. Off Shanal's body it lacked the power and substance it had carried when she'd worn it into the church last Saturday. It was nothing more than a pretty dress with maybe a few too many sparkles attached. He wondered if she wanted it back, and the dainty shoes set beneath it on the shoe rack.

A swell of impotent rage filled him, making him want to drag the gown from its hanger and cast it back on the floor where Shanal had left it. He swallowed against the urge to roar in disgust at the whole situation. The relief would be only temporary and yelling would do nothing whatsoever toward solving the problem. Shanal had chosen to go with Burton. Sure, there had been disturbing undercurrents between her and her fiancé—it didn't take an honors student to figure that out. What they hadn't said in front of him was certainly more interesting than what they had.

But how to get to the bottom of it, that was the question. Burton had to have some kind of leverage over Shanal. He just had to. Or did he? Maybe it was just that Raif preferred to believe that, since otherwise he'd be forced to conclude that Shanal had used him simply to make a point with her fiancé. He shoved the idea ruthlessly from his mind before it could bloom into anything else.

She was not like that. At least, she'd never been like that in all the years he'd known her. Besides, Ethan was a great judge of character and he certainly wouldn't call someone his best friend if she was the type of person to use another, to go so far as to sleep with him, simply to further her own agenda. And there'd been that sense of innocence about Shanal when they'd kissed and when they'd made love for the first time. That wasn't something you could fake.

Raif slammed the door of the wardrobe and strode from the room. He'd get to the bottom of this somehow.

Shanal shoved a pen behind her ear and rubbed at her eyes. Working late at the laboratory, going over and over the test results from their latest genetic experiment to increase the yield of a particular strain of vinafera hybrid, had done nothing to calm her mind or relieve the ever tightening noose of strain that trapped her. She pushed her chair back from her desk and stared out the window of her office into the darkness that lay beyond. How symbolic it was of her life at the moment, at least of her future, she thought with a shiver of foreboding.

When Burton had delivered her to her parents' home on Tuesday night last week, she'd felt exhausted and unwilling to talk. But sometime in the night she'd heard her mother up and moving about in the house, and she'd gone to her. Shanal still couldn't quite rid herself of the dreadful and overwhelming sense of guilt she'd felt as she'd seen her mother—her shoulders bowed, her skin gray with worry and her mouth a grim line as she'd paced back and forth. It was Shanal's fault her mom was unable to sleep even though she was exhausted from caring for her husband all day. All their problems could be solved if she'd just do one thing—marry Burton Rogers.

And she had a second chance now to put things right, even if doing so would probably kill every last dream and hope she'd ever had. She had to go through with it, though, for her father and for her mother. They'd done everything for her, given her every opportunity. Oh, sure, she knew that's what parents did for their beloved children. Yes, with love came sacrifice. But what of her love for them? If she could do anything, anything at all, to make her father's remaining time—whether it be months or years—as trouble free and comfortable as he'd worked to make her life from the day she was born, she would do it. It was that simple.

And that hard.

Burton had been civil since he'd brought her home—that was about the only term she could use to describe the cool politeness with which he greeted her each day as she'd arrived at work. She caught his reflection behind hers in the window now. It was as if thinking about him had helped him to materialize here in her office. She turned, ready to face him.

"You've been home a week now," he said calmly, but she could see the vein pulsing high on his forehead, at the edge of his hairline. She'd learned that was the marker that he was less than pleased. "I thought you might have made some effort to discuss our wedding by now."

"I…" Her voice trailed away. There was nothing to say.

"I've been more than reasonable, Shanal—I've given you a week to pull yourself together after your unfortunate behavior. But I think you can appreciate that I will not wait forever. I want you as my wife. Set a date."

There was a grim note of determination to his voice that sent a shiver down her spine. She held back a sigh and swiveled her chair around to face him.

"Twelfth of September," she said, as firmly as she could. She pulled her calendar up on her phone and scrolled through the dates. "But no fuss this time. Just something small."

He nodded. "Excellent. I'll make the arrangements. I'm glad to see you've come to your senses. The twelfth is perfect timing. I'll be back by then."

"Back? From where?" He hadn't mentioned anything about having to go away anywhere in the lead-up to their original wedding day.

"I'm needed at our facility in California. An urgent and unexpected matter. I leave tomorrow."

Shanal fought to hide her relief. Not having his oppressive presence around would be small compensation for the next few weeks, at least.

"A problem?" she asked.

"Nothing I can't handle," he replied smoothly.

He stepped forward and raised a hand to grip her chin and tilt her face upward, then bent down to kiss her. His lips were cold and smooth, so very much like the man himself. Despite his coaxing, she kept her mouth firmly closed. This was nothing like the warmth and slow burning need she'd shared with Raif. In fact, if two men could be polar opposites, then Burton and Raif were that. Instead of desire gently unfurling within her, she felt the sting of distaste. Instead of anticipation, she felt only dread.

She would submit when it was time, but right now, with the memory of Raif's kisses still so sweet and fresh in her mind, this embrace of Burton's was nothing but a travesty. She jerked back slightly as he suddenly released her and straightened, looking down upon her once more, his face impassive.

"See if you can't drum up a little enthusiasm for my touch while I'm gone, hmm? And I expect I don't have to tell you this, but stay away from Raif Masters."

And with that parting shot he was gone. He didn't need to verbalize a threat. She knew what would happen if she saw Raif again and Burton found out. All bets would be off the table and he'd follow through on his threats against her. As much as Burton Rogers coveted her, he wouldn't share her with anyone else—certainly not a second time.

He was not a man who liked to be thwarted. She knew her appeal to him had grown out of his need to surround himself with rare and beautiful things. The way he looked at her, as if she were a priceless artifact, made her feel more objectified than if he'd wolf-whistled every time he saw her. Her intelligence only served to make her more appealing to him, she knew for a fact. And as his wife, she'd never leave his employ. All of that played into his original reasons for proposing. And now, ever since the wedding day that wasn't, she got the sense that his competitiveness with Raif just made him more determined to "win" her away from his rival and lock her into marriage vows once and for all.

Despite the way everything inside her railed against Burton's dictates, she wouldn't be making any effort to see Raif again. He'd used her—he hadn't even attempted to deny it. And even more galling, she'd been his willing partner in that. The man had swamped her with feeling, with emotion. He had cut past all the clinical and careful ways she'd lived her life to date, and made her aware of everything with a clarity that had taken her breath away. And it had all happened so darn fast.

How could she trust it? She was the kind of person who measured everything twice, examined every minute detail over and over. Who took the greatest care before committing to a decision, whether it be work or social or even what shoes to wear with her outfit each morning.

Raif was the antithesis of that. He was impulsive and daring. Physical and creative. Her body burned anew as she remembered just *how* creative he could be. They'd spent only one intimate night together, and one equally intimate morning, learning one another's bodies as if they were maps to a pirate's bountiful treasure, but the memories they'd created burned with perpetual ferocity, making her nights ever since barren and empty by comparison.

Shanal let go of the breath she'd been holding. She'd thought the idea of marrying Burton before was impossible. Marrying him now was going to be a great deal more difficult than she had ever imagined. But she'd do it. She had no other choice.

Ten

Raif pulled up outside Shanal's parents' home. Shanal hadn't taken his calls last Friday at work, nor would she come to the phone over the weekend. An attempt to see her at Burton International had led to being escorted from the building by security—whether by Burton's dictate or Shanal's, he couldn't be sure.

There was nothing left but to try and catch her here, at home. Raif knew Mr. and Mrs. Peat were out because he'd just passed them in their specially modified car, heading the other way. He drummed his fingers on the steering wheel for a minute before grabbing the garbage sack he'd stowed on the seat beside him, and getting out the car. Bringing the Maserati probably hadn't been the best idea, but he'd realized that only after he'd shoved and squeezed the bag full of the foaming concoction of material that was Shanal's wedding dress into the trash bag and put it in the passenger seat beside him. And once he'd gotten it into the car, there was no way he was dealing with hauling it back out until it was time to pass it over once and for all.

Shanal's car was nowhere to be seen, but he knocked on the front door of the house anyway, and counted slowly under his breath, waiting for an answer. Nothing. Seconds later, he noticed her little hatchback slowing outside the house. From his vantage point on the front porch he saw the moment she recognized his car parked out front.

She pulled into the driveway and looked toward the front door, her face pale and her beautiful eyes huge as she saw him standing there. For a second he thought that she'd shove the car into Reverse and back out of there and away from him as fast as she could. Instead she appeared to hasten to get out the car. She all but ran the short distance to the front door.

A waft of her scent, that combination of spice and flowers that he would never again be able to smell without thinking of her, tantalized him. She looked tired. He'd bet good money that Burton was responsible for that, too. It made Raif want to physically remove Shanal from the man's noxious sphere. But, he reminded himself grimly, she'd made her choice and that choice had not been him.

"What are you doing here?" she asked in a fierce undertone, looking over her shoulder at the road—almost as if she was afraid she was being watched.

"I had to return this. I imagine you'll be needing it again soon?" He deliberately let the jibe fall from his lips.

She flinched as if the words had held more sting than he'd intended. "Thank you," she said stiffly, raising her eyebrows a little at the receptacle he'd chosen to return the dress in. She took the bag from him and then stood to one side as if, dress delivered and accepted, she now expected him to leave.

"And we need to talk," he continued.

"There's nothing to talk about. Please leave."

"Not until you answer at least one question."

"Fine," she huffed, her eyes drifting up and down the street before returning to his face. "Spit it out."

"Why are you marrying him?"

"Because I have to. You've asked your question. I've answered it. You can go now. If Burton knew you were here—"

"What?" he interrupted. "What would he do?"

"Please, Raif, just leave," she begged.

A sour taste filled Raif's mouth when he recognized the fear behind her words. "What? Can't you do anything without his approval? And you're telling me you want to *marry* him? Is he really the kind of man you want to be bound to for the rest of your life?"

"I've asked myself a lot of things, Raif, but it all comes back to the same thing. He's the man I'm going to marry."

Raif shoved a hand through his hair. "I just don't get it. Why him? You don't love him, I know that for a fact. A woman like you... Well, I doubt you'd have shared yourself with me the way you did if you actually had feelings for him. Unless...unless *you* were using *me*. Playing me off against him for some crazy reason. Was that what it was?"

If anything, her face paled even more. The garbage sack fell from her fingers and her eyes filled with tears. "Is that what you think? That I'd do something like that?"

"Is it true?"

She shook her head vehemently. "No, it's not. Now, I've answered more than one question. Consider the extras a bonus and please leave."

Shanal reached into her handbag and pulled out a house key. Her hand was shaking as she fitted it to the lock. Raif reached to take the key from her and finish the job, but she pulled away so quickly when his fingers brushed hers that the key fell to the floor. He bent to pick it up, and shoved it into the lock, giving it a sharp turn and pushing the door open. He extracted the key and made a show of handing it back to her carefully so that they didn't need to touch at all this time.

"I'm not going to let this go, Shanal. You ran away from him once."

"That was a mistake. Finding out you used me to get back at Burton helped me to realize what I need to do," she said breathlessly, and pushed past him to get inside the house.

"Shanal, really? Do you honestly think that what we shared together was about revenge?"

She sighed deeply. "No," she admitted with a huff of air, and started to close the door.

"I'm still here for you. Confused as hell about why you're doing this, but here for you. Do you understand me?"

"I don't need you, Raif. I have Burton. Goodbye."

The door shut in his face. He considered knocking on it, demanding she explain further, but he knew it would be futile. He went back to his car, and all the way home replayed her words over and over in his mind. Not once had she mentioned caring for Burton or, heaven forbid, loving him. So why the hell was she going through with this again?

Love was, or at the very least *should* be, the only

reason one person married another. Marriage was a lifetime commitment. It was the blending of two people to make a better whole. A combination of personalities that knitted together with one thread. It was the root stock of a family, the basis for generations to come. What sense was there in starting a relationship like that without a strong foundation of love in the place first?

As he pushed the Maserati the winding miles back to his home, Raif realized that, more than anything, he wanted a real, loving marriage—and he wanted it with Shanal. His foot eased a little on the accelerator as a new revelation filled him. He loved her, and probably had since he was a teenager. All those little barbs they'd flung at one another, on his side at least, had masked deeper feelings. Feelings he'd hidden after the embarrassment of her rejection all those years ago. But deep down, underneath it all, he loved her and, subconsciously at least, he hadn't been able to settle for anyone else. He'd been prepared to wait.

Accepting the knowledge brought a strange sense of peace, easing the turmoil of his thoughts. It was right. Maybe the timing hadn't been the best for them in the past, and by the looks of things, it certainly wasn't now, but Raif wasn't about to let her go. Initial failure had never discouraged him from striving to reach his goals before, and he wasn't about to let it knock him back now. Whether she knew it or not, the waiting was over.

Shanal Peat was his. He had only to convince her of that, to gain her full trust. Then and only then would she let him know the true reason why she was thinking about marrying Burton. She hadn't even been able to lie about her reason for marrying him. If she'd have said she loved him then maybe, just maybe, Raif might have stepped back.

He chewed the thought over in his mind and then barked a cynical laugh. Who was he kidding? There was no way on this earth he would accept that a woman as sensitive and vulnerable as Shanal could love a man like Burton Rogers. But could she love Raif? He certainly hoped so, because suddenly the idea of a life without her in it loomed very emptily ahead.

Shanal lifted her head in shock at the doctor's words. *"Pregnant?"*

A roaring sound filled her ears. She couldn't be pregnant. It just wasn't possible. She knew the doctor continued to talk to her, and somehow she must have responded, but she failed to grasp his words. She'd come to the surgery, on her mother's insistence, for a general checkup, because she'd been feeling off-color and over-tired these past few weeks. While Shanal was ready to blame her general malaise on the stress she was feeling with her wedding in only two weeks' time, not to mention her current workload, she was not prepared for this.

And then there were the daily calls from Burton, checking up on her even though she had a very strong suspicion he also had people watching her every movement. He'd dropped a bombshell last night, telling her he'd wrapped up his business early and would be home tomorrow. She'd hung up from the call and felt so ill with nerves at the prospect of seeing him again that she'd been forced to head straight for the bathroom as her stomach rejected its contents. She'd put it down to anxiety, but it seemed the cause was something far more alarming.

This morning, her mother had been insistent that she see her doctor, and Shanal had been lucky enough to fit into his schedule, thanks to a cancelation. Now this. Her hand automatically fluttered to her lower belly, to where a child was forming. Her baby—and Raif's.

This was unarguably the worst thing that could happen to her right now. There had been only the one time without protection. She'd been off the pill for just three days. She'd believed the odds of her becoming pregnant to be so remote as to be unsustainable, and yet here she was. Her head swam as she tried to adjust to the news. She was going to be a mother.

Fear and exhilaration battled with equal strength inside her. What on earth was she to do? She certainly couldn't marry one man while she was pregnant with another man's child. How was she going to tell either of them?

By the time she was outside the doctor's office and back in her car she was no clearer on what to do. She'd shoved the fistful of brochures the nurse had given her into her handbag without even looking at them. She couldn't push more information into her brain just yet. She was still struggling to accept the fact that her life was on the cusp of massive change at a level she'd never imagined.

"Your fiancé will be excited, I'm sure," the nurse had said with a cheerful smile and a knowing look at the ring Shanal had been forced to wear again.

Excited was not the word she would use, mainly because given the fact they'd barely done more than share several lukewarm kisses, Burton would know there was no chance the baby was his. He hadn't pressured her into anything more, saying he was happy to wait until their wedding night. The wedding night that had never happened. Her stomach clenched on that thought. The nurse was looking at her brightly, expecting a reply. Shanal could only murmur an indistinct sound in response. She dreaded the thought of his actual reaction. The last thing she wanted was to give the manipulative man beneath the courteous veneer another reason to tighten the leash he already had her on.

Shanal started the car and pointed it in the direction of her parents' home. Somehow she'd get through today. And then tomorrow, when Burton returned; she'd get through that, as well. She didn't want to think past that point because the variables were far too many and most of them too awful to even consider. One step at a time. That's what took her through her research and that's what would get her through the next twenty-four hours, too.

On Saturday, Shanal drove to Burton's inner-city apartment when she received his call to say he was home. He'd sounded pleased when she'd said she needed to see him, but she doubted he'd sound that way for long once he heard what she had to say. All the way up in the elevator, she twisted the strap of her handbag round and round, letting it go to unravel, then she'd start all over again. It was much like her stomach felt right now, she thought. Caught up in a coil of tension that would release momentarily, then wind back up. Each time tighter than before.

The door to Burton's apartment swung open before she could so much as raise her hand to press the bell.

"Come in," he said, leaning forward to kiss her, his expression of welcome freezing just a little when she averted her head so his lips grazed her cheek and not their intended target. "I've missed you, darling. Did you miss me, too?"

Oh, she had. She absolutely had. But not in the way he obviously hoped—more like how someone missed an aching tooth once it had been pulled. "It's been quiet without you," she said in a weak compromise.

He laughed, the sound forced and artificial in the soullessly beautiful, magazine-spread-style perfection that was his apartment. It had never bothered her before, but somehow now it felt empty of personality. More like a stage than a home and nothing at all like Raif's house, which, although modern, was furnished in a warm and comfortable manner. What she'd seen of it during her short time there, anyway.

"I'm flattered that you were in such a hurry to see me. Come, let me get you something. A cup of tea? Coffee?"

Her stomach lurched. "Maybe a glass of water."

He cast her an assessing glance. "Are you feeling well, Shanal? You're a little pale."

And here it was. Her opening. But she couldn't quite find the words. How did you tell your fiancé you were expecting another man's baby? And not just any man's, but the baby of the man he hated above all others. She'd realized that fact the day on the riverbank.

"I've been feeling a little unwell recently," she admitted, taking the glass of water he gave her and having a small sip.

"Nothing serious, I hope? Have you been to the doctor?"

He was all concern, on the surface at least. But she could see the hard glint in his eyes as he studied her, looking for signs of imperfection.

"No, it isn't serious—well, not in a life-threatening way at least," she said with a wry quirk to her lips. "And, yes, I've seen a doctor. He gave me some surprising news."

"News?" Burton dropped all pretense of civility. "Cut to the chase, Shanal. What's wrong with you?"

"Actually, nothing is *wrong*, per se. I'm just pregnant, that's all."

Eleven

Burton's face went pale, then suffused with vivid color as he digested her words. *"Pregnant?"*

"I know, it came as a surprise to me, too."

"A surprise. That's rich. We both know it's not my child. You haven't let me touch you."

"We agreed on that, Burton." She felt she had to point it out in her defense.

"Yes, but not because I thought you would let your passions overwhelm you and drive you to sleep with Raif Masters!" he spat in return.

Shanal flinched. Burton had never shown anger like this before. Sure, she understood he had to be very angry indeed at this news. It was a very unexpected wrinkle in the fabric of his plans. But it had happened. Now they needed to deal with it.

"You'll get rid of it, of course," he stated flatly.

"I beg your pardon?" Shanal couldn't quite believe what he'd said.

"I have chosen to accept the fact that you've slept with Raif Masters, however ill-advised it was, and move on. I will not, however, accept his bastard as a cuckoo in my nest. You *will* get rid of it," he ordered, his voice seething with revulsion, "and before the wedding."

"Rid of it? You mean—?"

"Yes, of course I mean an abortion. Let me be very clear, Shanal. I won't tolerate you continuing this pregnancy for a moment longer than necessary. Remember what you have at stake here. If you insist on going through with this pregnancy you can forget about the money you need so very much to help your parents, and you can forget about your position with Burton International. And let's not forget your restraint clause. I will invoke that if I have to. And you can be certain that once those two years are up, I will make sure you never get work in this field again into the bargain.

"Ask yourself, what do you really want? Hmm? The choice is yours. But if you choose me, then you do so without that man's brat inside you."

Fine tremors rocked her body. She couldn't believe what Burton was asking of her. Every particle within her vehemently rejected his ultimatum, but what other choice did she have? Her father couldn't work anymore. Her mother was now his full-time caregiver, and besides, she'd never worked outside the home. Even if she could find a job it would be unskilled and the pay would hardly make a dent in their living costs. For her entire married life her sole focus had been her husband and Shanal. If they could sell their home, sure, their debts would be cleared, but where would they live? What would they do to cover their living expenses? It was likely a moot point, anyway, with the mortgage that Burton now held over the property. They'd never be able to sell it with his interests registered against it.

Burton's stipulation was an all-or-nothing deal. If she married him, she continued with her work and provided the necessary security for her family, but that meant she'd have to give up the child of a man who'd done everything she'd asked of him without question, but who could do nothing to save her now.

"What's it to be, Shanal?" Burton pressed relentlessly.

Could she do what he asked? She swallowed against the lump in her throat and lifted her head to look at this man she'd agreed—not once, but twice—to marry.

In a voice that sounded foreign to her ears she replied, "I'll marry you."

A smile stretched across Burton's face and Shanal watched in horror, wondering how she'd ever thought him handsome.

"Don't you worry about the details, darling," he said with that crocodile smile. "I'll arrange everything. Besides, we can't have a baby ruining that pretty little figure of yours, can we?"

His words sent a chill through her. She could understand he wouldn't want Raif's child, but from what he'd just said, he didn't ever want to see her pregnant. "Burton, are you saying you don't want children at all?"

"When we're ready we can use a surrogate. I don't want anything to mar the perfection of you, Shanal. Not now, not ever. I remember the first time I saw you. I knew you had to be mine. I couldn't believe my luck when you interviewed for the position at the lab eighteen months ago. There was no way I was letting you go. Ours will be the perfect marriage and together we'll make Burton International the number-one research facility in the world."

Two things locked into her mind. First, that he'd planned to marry her all this time. And second, that she'd earned her role in the lab based on her looks rather than her qualifications. She'd never felt more trivialized in her life. The knowledge heightened her loathing of him.

Oblivious to her distress, Burton continued. "So, tell me, you are going to wear that exquisite gown again for our wedding, aren't you? I can't wait to see you in it once more."

By the time Shanal left his apartment she felt bruised inside. Through everything they'd discussed, she couldn't help feeling she was making the worst mistake of her life. Raif had tried to warn her months ago and she hadn't been prepared to listen. But then again, she had never seen the side of Burton that she'd seen today.

It was as if he were two distinct people—the charming, urbane, smiling gentleman boss on the one hand, and a calculating, controlling despot on the other. And she was linking herself to him, in marriage, forever. He didn't even really see her as a person, but more of an asset. This wasn't what she'd mentally signed up for when she'd first agreed to marry him. Although maybe, somewhere along the line, she'd subconsciously realized who Burton Rogers really was when she'd chosen to run away from the cathedral that day. If only that instinct had taken over before she'd agreed to his proposal in the first place.

How could she go through with this?

She thought about her parents, of her father wilting away in his wheelchair. Of her mother, burdened with his care.

How could she not?

* * *

On Monday morning, at work, she got a call to see Burton in his office. She smoothed her white coat with trembling hands and knocked on the door to his inner sanctuary.

"Come in," he answered, his muted voice sending a shiver down her spine.

"You asked to see me?" she said, as she stepped inside.

Burton had his back to her, surveying the impeccably landscaped grounds outside. Slowly he turned. Shanal looked at him and felt her skin crawl. Her hands curled into balls and she shoved them into the deep pockets of her white coat. Maybe if she could just focus on the pain of her fingernails embedding into her palms, she could fight back the swell of nausea assailing her that had absolutely nothing to do with her pregnancy.

"How are you today, darling?" he said with a smile that she noticed didn't touch his eyes.

"Busy." Her response was clipped and to the point. And it was true, she was incredibly busy in the lab. An intern had inadvertently corrupted important data on her most recent study and she'd been cross-referencing her notes all morning.

"Glad to see you're still taking your responsibilities to your work so seriously. Which leaves the other matter." Burton's mouth pulled into a frown of distaste.

She stared at him, refusing to acknowledge "the matter" in the same terms as he had couched them. Logically, she'd known that Burton wouldn't be happy with the news about the baby, but her mind emphatically rejected the idea that he could so clinically dismiss the child that even now formed within her.

"You'll be pleased to know I've been able to have

you scheduled at a private clinic the day after tomorrow. That gives you ten days to recover before our wedding."

"Wednesday? So soon?" she blurted.

"It doesn't pay to allow these things to linger," he said, all pretense of amiability now gone. "I'll pick you up in the morning and take you myself."

No doubt to ensure that she went through with it, she thought, nodding to indicate that she had heard.

"Is that all?" she said, now desperate to leave the oppression his presence had become.

"For now," Burton said, turning back to the view outside, dismissing her as if she was no longer of consequence now he'd made his dictate clear.

A phrase he'd mentioned on Saturday, about not wanting anything to mar the perfection of her, echoed in her mind. Was that all she was to Burton? An image of his idea of perfection? Something to be admired and brought out and displayed at will? She'd honestly thought, even though she didn't love him, that they could possibly make a go of marriage. If she hadn't believed that from the very start she would never have agreed to marry him. But now, that looked less and less likely. And yet how on earth was she to extricate herself from this dreadful mess? He held all the cards and he'd made no bones about playing them to punish her if she thwarted him in any way.

She entered her office and closed the door firmly behind her before sinking into her chair and staring with blind eyes at the data displayed on her computer screen. Sure, she could tell Raif—in fact she *should* tell Raif— about the baby. She knew without doubt that she and the child would be gathered up in the embrace of his family in an instant. But what of her parents? What of her career? If she didn't do as Burton said, she'd save a potential life but destroy every other person and thing in her world that mattered.

What the hell was she going to do?

Shanal woke with a dreadful sense of loss on Wednesday morning. She'd barely slept and she felt weak and vulnerable as she prepared herself for the visit to the clinic. Burton would be here any moment and she had to be ready, but she struggled to find the motivation to wash and dress and gather her few things together. Doggedly, she pushed on, hoping she could be gone before her parents rose for the day. She had no wish to face them before the procedure. She couldn't bear to tell them any of it—about the pregnancy, or the abortion—because it would only expand the guilt her father already wore like a heavy yoke around his neck. It was better that they knew nothing about this.

The flash of Burton's lights as he turned into the driveway propelled her out the front door.

"All set?" he asked, as she got into his BMW.

She nodded, unable to speak. This was wrong, so wrong.

He reached across and patted her on the knee. "Don't worry, Shanal. Everything will be okay once it's over."

But would it? She'd still be tied to a man who was more ruthless than she'd ever expected. A man who lived to his own agenda without a thought or a care for others. A man who had blackmailed her into staying with him. Raif had tried to warn her, but she hadn't listened, hadn't seen what he'd been talking about. And now an innocent life would be lost because of it.

How many people had Burton hurt in his quest for perfection? Shanal had always admired how he didn't waver on the level of his standards. In fact, she'd been proud to work for a man who never accepted less than the best. It was how she'd worked her entire life. Always reaching to set the bar higher, to ensure that her marks were that much better, the results of her research unquestionable. They hadn't been so different, had they?

Nonetheless, there was an edge to Burton that she'd completely misunderstood. She'd thought it was a sign of his quest for excellence, but now it only seemed to be indicative of his quest to dominate.

They completed the journey in silence. Burton escorted her from the car to the admitting area and bent to kiss her on the cheek before he left.

"Call me when you're done and I'll come back for you," he said. "You're doing the right thing. Our life is going to be perfect together, Shanal. Trust me on this."

Perfect? She swallowed back the bitterness that rose in her throat. Perfect was lazy days on a houseboat on the Murray River. Perfect was a passionate night in the arms of Raif Masters. Her eyes filmed with unshed tears as she turned to confirm her details with the nurse waiting to admit her. She felt Burton leave, the air around her lightening in his absence.

The nurse was compassionate and professional, briskly showing Shanal through to the room where she'd change into her hospital gown, and discussing what would happen next. After some minor tests, an examination and a brief scan, she would be third on the list that morning. The procedure itself would be short, her recovery would include up to two hours under observation afterward, and then she could go home and rest.

It wasn't until the scanning equipment was brought in and Shanal bared her stomach that she knew for certain she couldn't go through with this. While her baby was no more than a blueberry-size bundle of multiplying cells at this point, he or she was still *her* baby and, she realized with increasing certainty, she wanted this baby with all her heart.

"No!" she said, pushing the sonographer's hand away. "I'm not doing it. I'm keeping my baby."

"Are you certain, Miss Peat? It's not unusual for you to feel undecided about this," the nurse said, her face a mask of compassion.

"I've never been more certain of anything," she answered. She sat up and wiped the gel from her stomach with her hospital gown. "I'm going home and I'm keeping my baby."

When the taxi deposited her back on the driveway at her house Shanal could feel only relief. She'd deal with Burton later. First, she had to tell her mum and dad about the baby.

Her parents were at the kitchen table when she let herself inside.

"You're back from work early, *pyaari beti*. Is everything okay?"

Beloved daughter. Shanal smiled fleetingly at her mother's endearment. While her mum had embraced her new Australian lifestyle over thirty years ago with the same love and commitment she showed to her Australian husband, she was at heart still Indian and often peppered her conversation with an odd mix of Hindi and English that left many people scratching their heads.

"I need to speak with you both. Do you have time?"

She sat at the table and accepted the cup of tea her mother had automatically poured for her.

"What…else would…we be doing?" her father asked in his stilted speech. "We're here…for you. What's… wrong?"

His struggle to form words seemed worse than usual and Shanal exchanged a look with her mother. Yet another advancement in the illness that was, inch by inch, taking her father's life away. Even so, there was nothing wrong with his mind and she needed to talk to them both. Initially, she didn't know where to begin, but eventually she took a deep breath and started with the day she'd run from her wedding. Her parents, to their credit, said very little during her recitation. But she felt her mother's cry of dismay as if it was a physical thing when she mentioned Burton's insistence on the termination.

"So you see, I couldn't go through with it. Which leaves me in a very difficult position."

"Do you love Raif?" her mother asked.

Shanal felt her breath hitch as she allowed the idea to expand in her mind. Love him? She knew she was deeply attracted to him. It was something she'd fought for so many years it had become second nature. Right up until he'd become her knight in shining armor and whisked her away from a marriage she hadn't wanted, to a retreat where she could hide from her problems. The urge to kiss him had come from a place deep inside her. Their lovemaking had brought the kind of fulfillment she'd always sought in her life, and the kind that had been lacking in her few relationships so far. So, did she love Raif? The tightness in her chest loosened and warmth swelled and filled its place.

"I don't know," she said. If she acknowledged how she felt about him that would only make marrying Burton all the more difficult and all the more hopeless. And it would leave her all the more susceptible to being hurt if he didn't share her feelings, too. "I think I might."

"Then marry Raif," her mother said bluntly. "He does know about the baby, doesn't he?"

"It's not that simple," Shanal replied, her voice soft and her eyes now fixed on her father. "I can't rely on him, Mum. He used me to get back at Burton."

"Did he really?" her mother asked, getting up to brew another pot of tea. "From what you've said, it seems to me that the thought might have crossed his mind initially, but it certainly didn't stay there."

"That's what he said," Shanal admitted.

"Then I see no reason for you not to believe him. Did he lie to you? Did he hide the truth from you when you asked him?"

"No, he didn't, but there are other things to consider. If I don't marry Burton, I will lose my position with Burton International. And there's a restraint clause in my contract. If I leave Burton International, I am legally unable to work in the same field anywhere in Australia for at least two years. It was stupid of me not to realize the long-term implications of that."

Understanding filled her father's eyes as he digested the message hidden in her words. Understanding that was swiftly followed by remorse. She was not about to put it in so many words, but the three of them knew that without her income they'd all be destitute.

"I just don't know what to do anymore."

Shanal stood up and took her cup of tea through to her childhood bedroom. There, surrounded by so many reminders of her past, she tried to digest the truth about her feelings for Raif. Theoretically, it should be so simple. She could just tell Burton the truth, that she planned to keep her baby and that she wouldn't be marrying him. How hard could that be?

But then the look on her father's face came back to

haunt her. He'd been through hell since the medical-negligence compensation claim. He hadn't fought it, instead taking full responsibility for the damage he'd done—for the death he'd caused by trying to soldier through his illness without telling his peers. Her dad's shame and sorrow were a heavy burden for them both. He was a man used to being larger than life and a powerful force in the health field, along with supporting his family. The physical and mental toll the whole incident had taken was huge, accelerating the symptoms of his illness.

She looked up as she heard his wheelchair at her door.

"Will…you be…okay?" he asked, forming his words carefully.

Shanal looked at her father, his eyes still bright with intelligence and shining with the love he bore for her.

"Yes, Dad, I'll be okay." *Somehow.* "We'll *all* be okay, I promise."

Her father looked up at her. He laughed, a dry crackling sound that held little warmth. "Your mother reckons…she's going…to get a job."

Shanal shook her head. "No, she can't. You need her here at home."

When Shanal had learned about her father's illness, they'd realized that there would come a point when he'd need full-time nursing care. Her mother had been adamant that if anyone was to care for her husband, it would be her for as long as she could manage. Shanal had used some of her own savings to make alterations to the house so her father could remain at home and maneuver safely in his wheelchair.

Shanal's mum appeared in the doorway, resting her hands on her husband's shoulders and giving them a squeeze. Her features were drawn into a tight mask and her jaw was set with determination.

"Either way, *pyaari beti,* you can't carry our responsibilities on your own, not with a baby now to consider, as well. We don't want you to put yourself through hardship for us."

"We…love you," her father added. "You must…do… what's right for…you."

Shanal watched as her parents left her room, marveling at the way their love for one another was still as rock solid as it had ever been. She wanted that for herself now more than ever—that kind of love that endured through good times and bad, through sickness and in health. She wouldn't have that with Burton. She knew that. Could she honestly let herself live without it?

Her hand rested against her lower belly. She had responsibilities here—to her unborn babe and to her parents. She had to go ahead with her marriage to Burton. She simply had no other choice. And when he discovered that she hadn't gone through with the termination, well, she'd just have to cross that bridge when she reached it.

Twelve

Raif paced the tasting room at The Masters vineyard, oblivious to the expression of amusement on his cousin Ethan's face.

"Of course I love her. Do you think for a second that I'd be this wound up if I didn't?" Raif raged.

"Well, why don't you do something about it," Ethan drawled, as he leaned back in his chair and twirled the stem of a glass of Shiraz between his fingers.

"Like what? She refuses to see me, she won't answer my calls, I'm banned from Burton International—"

"Seriously?" Ethan choked on a laugh. "Banned from her workplace?"

Raif clenched his teeth together as he struggled to get his frustration under control. "It's no laughing matter."

Ethan sobered, all humor gone as he sat up straighter in his chair. "Then you have to find a way. If she's that important to you, then you have to go get her. You spirited her away once, and I have to say I commend you for that. You can do it again, surely. I still can't believe it, though. You and Shanal."

"Why is that so strange?"

"You've always been at one another. If she said black, you'd say white. If you said organic, she'd just about write a treatise on why the use of chemicals was vital for strong healthy growth."

Raif had to admit it, on the surface it had looked as if they couldn't bear one another. But when they'd been alone together on the boat, the animosity and bickering had vanished. They'd been happy together—the happiest he'd ever been. And he knew, to his soul, that she felt something for him. Love? Well, he could only hope. He just knew that she was marrying Burton for all the wrong reasons, whatever they were. She'd had reasons for running from the wedding last time, too. Reasons that, while she hadn't shared them with him, had made her desperate to leave the cathedral behind. Reasons that had given her nightmares that first night on the boat. Whatever she felt for Burton, it certainly wasn't love. If anything, it looked more like fear.

"What if you get her over here for lunch with you and Isobel, and then leave us to it. Would you do that for me?" Raif asked, latching on to the suggestion like a drowning man.

"Are you asking if I'm prepared to damage a friendship of fifteen years by tricking her into seeing you?"

Raif pinched the bridge of his nose and closed his eyes for a minute. It was asking too much of his cousin to do this. It was unfair. But then again, this whole situation was unfair. And beneath it all he still had the feeling that something about the whole thing was twisted. As if Burton was manipulating them all. There was only one answer to Ethan's question. Raif opened his eyes, let his hand drop back to his side.

"Yes," he said.

His cousin nodded in acknowledgment and sighed. "Fine, I'll do it. But don't blame me if it all blows up in your face."

"I won't," Raif assured him, even though deep down he had no such confidence.

Without saying another word, Ethan reached for his mobile phone and keyed in Shanal's number. After some idle chatter he got to the point, inviting her to lunch on the coming Sunday—one day shy of a week before her new wedding date.

"It's done," Ethan said. "She'll be here at midday. I suggest you come about an hour after that."

"I'll be here," Raif promised.

Sunday came, delivering one of those perfect early spring days filled with sunshine and a top temperature in the low sixties. Even so, Raif felt chilled as he got out of his car and walked toward the main house, where Ethan and Isobel were entertaining Shanal. She wouldn't be pleased, he knew that. No doubt she thought she'd effectively seen the last of him that day he'd returned her wedding dress, but if that was the case she'd failed to factor in the Masters family's resilience and determination to reach their goals.

He walked around to the back veranda of the house, which accommodated most of his family in its widespread wings to the sheltered spot where Ethan had texted him earlier to find them. Raif could hear the delicate sound of Shanal's laughter as he drew nearer. Laughter that cut short as she saw him step up onto the covered wooden deck.

"Ethan?" she asked, turning to his cousin.

"He needed to see you, Shanal. I'm sorry."

Isobel looked from one to the other and back again. "Is there something I'm missing here?"

"No, nothing," Shanal insisted, but Ethan spoke over her.

"I'll tell you, inside," he said to his wife, rising from his chair and offering her his hand.

With another sharp look at Raif and then Shanal, Isobel took her husband's hand. Raif waited until they were both inside and the door had closed behind them.

"I don't know what you hope to achieve by this, Raif. I told you, I can't see you anymore. We have nothing to say to each other."

"Can't see me? Or don't want to see me? They're two very different things, don't you think?" he said, lowering himself to sit beside her at the beautifully laid table. "I don't understand why you have to marry Burton."

"It's none of your business, Raif. Please, just leave me alone."

"Oh, Shanal, that's where you're so very wrong. It's entirely my business."

Her eyes flicked up to meet his, a tormented expression clearly evident. Raif's heart squeezed painfully that he had to be the one putting her through this.

"If you're going to marry anyone, it should be me. I love you, Shanal, and I believe, if you're honest with yourself, you love me, too."

She shook her head sadly. "No, don't do this to me, Raif. It's not fair."

"Not fair? Isn't denying yourself the truth unfair, too? I think it is. Especially when that truth is what we mean to one another."

Shanal drew herself upright in her chair. "You're

mistaken. We had a fling. A very *brief* fling," she re-iterated. "That's all."

Raif held back a sigh. She was going to fight him on this to the bitter end, wasn't she? Well, if she thought he'd tuck his tail and run she had another think coming. He'd waited this long, he wasn't going to wait any longer. He loved and respected her too much for that. "We both know that's a lie. You're not that kind of woman and it was way more than a fling."

She smiled. "You think not? Well, I have news for you. You don't know me as well as you think you do. I'm tired of playing games and of being some kind of toy to be fought over between you and Burton. I know you don't like him. How do I know you're not saying you love me just to get back at him again? You two were always competitive, even back in your school days, from what I've been told. Clearly that hasn't changed."

"It's more than that. Way more. He's not the right man for you."

"Like he wasn't for Laurel, either? And yet she chose him."

Raif felt the barb strike home, but it only served to make him even more determined. "And look what happened to her, Shanal."

"It was an accident."

"It was carelessness. Burton's deliberate carelessness, I'm sure. It couldn't have been anything else."

"The inquest found otherwise. He was exonerated," she persisted.

"He lied. That's the way he operates, can't you see that? He'll say whatever he needs to, and pay whoever he needs to, to get what he wants."

Didn't she *want* to understand? Raif fought the urge to strangle something, or someone—preferably

Rogers—and dragged his focus back to the woman in front of him. Everything he said was the truth, but still she fought back.

Shanal huffed a derisive snort. "Of course you'd say something like that. But then, you're not all that different, are you?"

"Burton is all about the chase, Shanal. He likes the hunt, the capture. The win. Do you really think he loves you? He doesn't. He loves the *idea* of you."

Shanal pushed her chair away from the table. "I think I've heard enough. Either you go or I do."

Raif put out a hand to stop her from getting up. "Shanal, please reconsider. It's not too late."

She looked down at his hand on her arm, then raised her eyes to his again. "I've made my decision, Raif. You have to live with that."

Knowing that anything else he said now would be a waste of time, Raif loosened his hold on her. "Don't get up. I'll go. But I'm not giving up on you, Shanal. Not for a second. Whether you believe me or not, I love you. What I want more than anything is for you to be happy—and since I know you'd never find happiness with Burton, I'm not going to stop trying to put an end to this wedding."

"Raif, you're wasting your time."

"That's for me to decide," he said, and he turned to go.

He couldn't quite remember when he'd made the decision to drive into the city, but he knew exactly why when he pulled the Maserati up outside Burton's apartment block.

"We need to talk," he said into the intercom in the foyer, after buzzing Burton's apartment.

"By all means," replied the silky smooth voice of the man he'd grown to detest more than any other.

Inside Burton's apartment, Raif found himself holding on to his rage by a thread.

"So, to what do I owe the pleasure of your visit?" Burton said, after leading him into a sitting room that was more a testament to his ability to collect beautiful things than it was a place to relax.

"Let her go."

"I beg your pardon. I'm not sure I understand what you're talking about."

Raif wanted nothing more than to wipe the smug look off Burton's face. "You know full well that I mean Shanal. Let her go."

"She comes to me of her own free will," Burton replied. "If she wanted to stay with you, surely she wouldn't have terminated your baby just this week."

Bile rose, hot and sharp, in Raif's throat. "My baby?"

"Yes," Burton drawled. "I took her to the clinic last Wednesday myself. Such an unfortunate side effect of your little dalliance together, but easily dispensed with. It's a good thing I'm a forgiving man. Now that little mess is tidied up, Shanal and I can move forward. We'll make quite the dynamic duo, don't you think?"

Little mess? It took every ounce of Raif's considerable control not to take Burton by the throat and choke him for his lies. But was it a lie? Only one person could tell him that and she wasn't willing to talk to him again. She'd told him there was nothing left to say. Did that mean she really had gone through with it?

Why hadn't she told him about the baby? She had to know he'd stand by her, didn't she? Goodness only knew Raif had tried to make that clear to her often enough. Rage suffused him. At Burton for being the supercilious grasping spawn he was, at Shanal for refusing to see the real person behind the smiling fiancé she planned to pledge her life to, and for the unborn child he hadn't even had the chance to know about and would now never have the chance to meet.

He could barely speak. Burton Rogers had now effectively destroyed the lives of two people, Laurel and now Raif's baby, who should have been able to count on him for anything. Two people he'd loved, or would have loved if given half a chance. He spun on his heel and stalked to the door of the apartment.

"What? Not stopping for a drink, old friend?" Burton taunted from behind him.

But he wasn't listening anymore. He had let this happen and he had to admit the worst of his rage was for himself. For his inability to prevent Burton from destroying yet another life. Well, he'd failed, twice now. There was no way he'd fail again. Whatever it took, whatever he had to do, Shanal would not marry Burton Rogers next Saturday.

Raif forced himself to drive slowly back to his house. He had to get control of this fury that held him tight in its grip. He had to deconstruct what Burton had told him, to take it apart piece by piece and examine it carefully. Now, more than ever, it was vital he not rush at things like a bull at a gate. He'd done that with Shanal and met only resistance. There had to be more beneath all this.

As he sat in an easy chair staring out at the vineyard, *his* vineyard, he mulled over everything that had happened in the past few weeks. Trying to peer beneath the layers to find the truth at the core. Through it all, he could only see the woman Shanal was. Focused, dedicated and loyal to a fault.

Was that where the problem lay? Her loyalty? To Burton, maybe? He was her boss. Even as the idea bloomed in his mind he cast it aside. No, he had seen no indication of loyalty in Shanal's behavior when Burton had come to take her away. Loyalty to her family, maybe? Raif had been shocked to see her father accompany her down the aisle in a wheelchair. Someone had whispered something about his illness, motor neuron disease, in hushed tones as they'd gone past. Raif had had no idea Curtis Peat was in such bad shape.

Was it desperation to be married before her father died? Was that what drove her? Surely she knew Raif would offer marriage himself if they had a baby on the way. Ideas tumbled around in his head until he was almost dizzy with them. Perhaps it was her parents who had loyalty to Burton, who had chosen him as Shanal's suitor? But while Mrs. Peat was traditional in some ways, Raif couldn't believe she'd push her daughter into an arranged marriage. Not when it was well known that the Peats themselves had been a love match.

Yet Raif couldn't help thinking that her parents were the key to understanding the situation in some way. Shanal was close to her parents, there was no question of that. But what would be so important to their happiness that she'd sacrifice her own to ensure it? It couldn't be money. The Peats were an affluent family. Before her father's early retirement he'd had a very successful private practice as a cardiovascular surgeon.

So what the hell was it?

It was growing dark when he finally moved and got himself something to eat from the kitchen. But food did little to fill the aching sense of loss at the idea of a child gone before he could know about it. He scraped off his plate into the garbage, most of his meal uneaten, and shoved the plate in the dishwasher before heading to bed.

There, he lay in the dark of a starless night, lost in the many variables and possibilities that presented themselves. Vignettes from his and Shanal's time on the river rose in his thoughts again and again, to torment him. Her trust in him from the start, her asking him to stay. The night they'd spent together locked in passion so deep, so everlasting—at least he'd thought so at the time—that it had left an indelible imprint on his heart.

He loved her. It was pure and simple. And he wanted her in his life, forever. She could be clinical and almost scarily intelligent, but then on the flip side she was warm and compassionate, as well. No matter how he viewed the woman he'd known for half his life, he couldn't see her doing what Burton had suggested.

Which meant that possibly, hopefully, she hadn't gone through with it. Maybe Burton had it wrong. Maybe she still carried his child. There was only one person who could tell him, and he'd make certain she did as soon as he could see her again.

Thirteen

Shanal took her time getting ready to go out to The Masters for dinner. She'd initially turned the invitation down. It was a weeknight, she'd protested when Isobel had phoned to ask her to come over, and she was very busy at work. But Isobel had cut straight through her objections and to the heart of why she didn't want to go, and had told her that while Raif would be there, he'd been warned to be on his best behavior and not leave her in the same state she'd been last Saturday when he'd gone.

She lifted a hand to apply her eyeliner, having to pause and take a breath when her fingers shook slightly at the prospect of seeing him again. Could she do it? Deep down, she craved the sight of him, but every time she saw him made it that much more unpalatable to think about going through with her marriage to Burton. But surely she'd be able to keep her distance from Raif for just one night. The whole Masters family would be at the gathering. She knew them all well, and as Ethan's friend, had been a part of these types of gatherings for years. How difficult could it be? she reasoned with herself. Either way, Raif could hardly abduct her from his family home in front of his relatives.

Last Saturday, he'd said he wouldn't let her go. What exactly had he meant by that? If he intended to try and change her mind again, he was definitely running out of time. Her rescheduled wedding was in only three days' time.

Her tummy did that all too familiar flip at the thought, warning her that she was going to be sick. She fought back the nausea, gripping the bathroom basin until her fingers ached—their pain distracting her from the roiling sensation deep inside.

She heard the whir of her father's chair as it passed the bathroom.

"You all…right?" he asked from the doorway, enunciating his words with care.

"Sure, Dad. Just getting ready to go to The Masters for dinner."

"That's…nice. You work too…hard. You…deserve a break."

And so did he, she reminded herself in the mirror as he wheeled away again. He deserved a break from the guilt that plagued him every day over the medical error that had killed his patient, and from the ill-fated decisions he'd made about his investments. He deserved a break from the illness that took away his control over his life one piece at a time. And most of all, he deserved a break from the relentless fear that they'd lose the house over their head if she didn't go through with her marriage to Burton. Of all the horrors that her dad faced as his disease slowly claimed what was left of his body, this was the one thing that she could help with. She could make that single fear go away. And she would.

With that thought clear in her mind, Shanal finished applying her makeup and twisted her hair up into a loose chignon. There, she was ready for anything, she thought as she eyed her reflection. No one needed to know about the turmoil that alternately slithered and coiled in the pit of her stomach, every waking hour. She could only hope the tension wasn't harming her baby. She placed a hand over her still-flat tummy as a surge of protectiveness shot through her. She would allow *nothing* to hurt her child, no matter what Burton said or did.

She was the last to arrive at the gathering. She smiled her hello to Ethan's aunt Cynthia, who presided like some matriarchal queen over these evenings, and kissed Ethan on the cheek as he came forward to welcome her. Raif's parents must still be overseas, Shanal thought as she scanned the room, her eyes skimming over the man himself quickly. She knew the second he was aware of her presence there, and from the corner of her eye noted his movement as he excused himself from talking to Isobel.

"Do you want to talk with Raif," Ethan asked at her side, "or would you rather I head him off?"

"No, it's okay," Shanal responded, her heart beating like a trapped bird in her chest. "We need to be able to be civil with one another."

"Civil?" Ethan huffed a quiet laugh. "He doesn't look as if he has civil on his mind." But respecting her wishes, he stepped back. "I'll be just over there if you need me."

"Thank you," she said, swallowing hard. "But I'm sure I'll be fine."

She had mere seconds to shore up her defenses and then Raif was right there in front of her.

"I'm glad you came tonight," he said simply.

"I wasn't going to let the thought of you scare me away."

She knew her response was blunt, offensive even, but she also knew that if she was to get through this evening she needed to maintain the upper hand.

"Like I said," Raif said, with a smile that made his eyes glitter dangerously. "I'm glad you came. We need to talk."

She sighed in exasperation. "Raif, we've said all there needs to be said. Can't you just accept defeat? I'm marrying Burton on Saturday and that's final."

"Sweetheart, we can do this in front of my family or we can do this in private. Your choice."

There was something in his tone that made her spine stiffen. "Look," she started, "I told Ethan I'd be fine with you here, that we could be civil. If I thought for one minute that you'd be anything else, I wouldn't have come."

"Oh, I'm being civil." His voice was clipped, as if he'd clenched his jaw and was biting his words out in tiny chunks. "More civil than you realize. So, tell me about the baby."

A chill ran the full length of her spine. "B-baby?" she gasped.

"Yes, *our* baby, if I'm to believe your fiancé."

Shanal looked at Raif in horror. Burton had told him about the baby? If that was the case, he would have told Raif about the abortion, as well. That would go a long way toward explaining the anger that vibrated off him right now.

She shuddered. She hadn't wanted it to come to this, but now it seemed she had no choice. Could she maybe let him go on believing the baby was gone? No, she knew she couldn't. It was not only unfair to him, but grossly unfair to the child she carried. Raif deserved to know. Her mind fractured into a hundred scattered thoughts. If he knew that she was still pregnant, though, what would he do? Would he tell Burton that she hadn't gone through with the abortion, after all? Would she lose that final chance to save her parents from home-lessness, and keep her own job? She had to find out.

"Is there somewhere private—?"

"Come with me," he said, taking her by the elbow and leading her from the salon where they'd gathered for predinner drinks.

Ethan looked up and started toward them when he saw Raif begin to lead her away, but she mouthed, "It's okay," and he halted in his tracks. A look of concern was still on his face as Raif closed the door behind them.

He led her a few doors down the wide, wood-paneled corridor into a room she recognized as the library. She'd always loved it in here. The high ceiling looked as though it was held up by all the knowledge and stories held in the books that lined the tall shelves on all walls. A pad-ded window seat beckoned the avid reader, who had the choice of reading there or in one of the comfortable, deep armchairs that flanked the large fireplace.

"Private enough for you?" he asked, as he closed the heavy door behind them with a thud.

"Thank you," she answered, wrapping her arms about her as if she could somehow protect herself from what she had to say.

"Is it true?" he asked.

"Is what true?"

"Don't play games with me, Shanal. You're better than that. You know how I feel about family. How important it is to me. Were you or were you not pregnant with my child?"

She couldn't find the words to tell him the exact truth, and instead just nodded. The instant she did Raif paled, and a look of grief so raw, so painful it tore at her heart, crossed his face.

"Raif, no!" she cried, rushing to him and reaching up to cup his face with her hands. "It's not what you think."

He pulled away roughly. "Don't. Just don't. You can't console me on this, Shanal. You made a decision about something that affected both of us without telling me anything. If I hadn't brought it up tonight, I never would have known, would I? You had no right to do that."

"But I didn't do it. Please, you have to believe me. I didn't go through with the procedure. Burton doesn't know. I'm still pregnant with your baby."

"What are you saying? That you didn't have the… the…" His voice trailed away, as if he couldn't quite bring himself to even say the word.

"I couldn't do it." She couldn't help shuddering a little at her next thought. "Burton will be furious when he finds out."

"Burton has nothing to do with this."

"But he does!" she cried out. "I'm marrying him on Saturday. He doesn't want your baby in our marriage, and can you blame him for that? Would you want his if the situation was reversed?"

"You're kidding me, right? You're comparing me to him?" Raif shook his head. "You really don't know me at all, do you? If you were marrying me and carrying

his baby, I would still do my very best by that child because, no matter what, it would be a part of *you* first.
A child can't choose its parents, but parents can make
all the difference in the life of a child."

Shanal felt her entire body sag at his words. She had
misjudged him and she owed him an apology for that.

"Raif, I'm sorry. I shouldn't have spoken to you like
that."

"Too right you shouldn't. But that's got nothing to
do with this situation, with us. You can't marry him,
can't you see that? This baby, *our* baby," he said with a
wealth of emotion in his voice. "It changes everything."

She shook her head. She was so dreadfully trapped.
She'd promised her father she'd make everything right
for him and her mum. She couldn't let them down now.
She couldn't abandon them.

"I have to marry him, Raif."

"*Have* to?"

"You don't understand," she cried, her voice breaking
as the pressure and responsibility threatened to swamp
her like a mud slide rapaciously consuming everything
before it.

"Then explain it to me. Tell me why," he demanded,
frustration and anger creeping into his voice.

She wrapped her arms tighter around her body and
shook her head, her eyes blurring with tears. She closed
them, not wanting to see the confusion and hurt on
Raif's face a second longer. Not wanting to see the questions in his eyes that only she could answer. But they
weren't her answers to give. They were her father's, and
she knew his pride couldn't take any more. With his
health so precarious now, another blow would merely
hasten his inevitable death. She couldn't bear to have
that on her conscience.

Strong arms wrapped around her from behind and the warmth of Raif's body filtered through her clothing to her skin. She hadn't realized how cold she was until she felt his heat and his comforting touch.

"It'll be okay, Shanal. I'll make it okay for you, but you have to let me in. I'm working in the dark here until you tell me what kind of hold Burton has on you."

His words penetrated the sorrow in her mind. What kind of hold Burton had on her? What would make him ask a question like that? She asked him.

Raif's sigh was deep and she felt it all the way through to her bones. He turned her around in his arms so she was facing him.

"Burton Rogers is the kind of guy who gets what he wants. By fair means or by foul. I'm guessing he's gotten you by foul, am I right?"

She didn't so much as blink.

"Shanal," Raif coaxed. "I meant what I said last Sunday. I love you. I want to make everything right for you, but you have to tell me what's wrong so I can fix it. I want there to be an *us*. A future with you and our baby."

The authenticity in his words, in his delivery of them, pierced the shell around her, making her want to dream that he could be right. But Burton held all the cards in this particular game. If Shanal could have seen a way clear to leave him for good by now, she would have.

"It's impossible," she said, her voice so quiet that Raif had to bend his head closer to hear her. "He controls everything, Raif. You know what he's like. He doesn't make mistakes, not when it comes to getting something he wants. There's no way out of this for me."

"There's always a way out," Raif said, determination clear in every syllable. "Tell me, why does he have such a hold over you?"

She had to tell him. The burden of bearing it all on her own for so long was simply too much. Slowly, she began, going back five years to her father's motor neuron diagnosis, to his negligence, to his guilt and shame.

"I don't mean to sound callous," Raif said when she paused. "But didn't your father have insurance for that?"

"He did, and the settlement at the time was a generous one. But how do you make up for taking a life—a man's future? It tormented Dad. If he hadn't operated that day—if he'd told another consultant about his illness and admitted that he shouldn't be operating anymore—that patient might still be alive. He'd still be a loved and valued, contributing member of his family. Dad felt he owed it to the man's wife and kids to make sure they had monetary stability at the very least—that there would be money available for the children if they wanted to attend university, that his widow would have no financial concerns about loan repayments or being forced back to work just to provide for her kids. So he took out a loan using his home as security—a very large loan, thinking he could pay it back when his investment portfolio matured."

Understanding lit in Raif's eyes. "And he was one of the affected parties in that Ponzi scheme that made the headlines a couple of years ago, wasn't he? Did he lose everything?"

She nodded. "They had some funds aside, separate from the investment accounts, which they used to meet their loan repayments for a while, and to live on. I gave up my apartment and moved back home to help them out financially, and to give my mum some assistance with Dad's care."

"Could your mum and dad not sell the house? Move somewhere smaller, maybe?"

"We considered it, but we'd already done alterations

to the house to accommodate Dad's mobility issues. Besides, he's lost so much already, Raif. I promised him he'd be able to stay in his home right up until the end, and that I'd look after him and Mum. He's counting on me."

"So where does Burton come into this?" Raif asked.

"One night, when I was working late, Burton caught me at a weak moment. I broke down and told him about our financial troubles. He offered to make everything all right. He'd personally take over the mortgage on my parents' house, repay their loan to the bank and provide a living allowance for them, on one condition."

"That you marry him."

She nodded.

"And what will he do if you don't marry him?"

"He will expose my father's negligence case to the media. The settlement was private and the facts of the case were never brought into the public eye. Also, Burton said he'd evict them from their home. Raif, the private shame of that case is already driving Dad into an early grave. I know he did wrong, making the decision to continue to operate that day, but he's done everything he possibly can to make amends. He stopped practicing, stopped everything that gave him purpose in his life. That error of judgment aside, his reputation, the *good* work he'd done up until his retirement, is all he has left.

"And there's something else. Burton made it clear to me that if I don't marry him, I will lose my position with Burton International. And aside from my two-year restraint clause, he assured me that I would never be able to find work here in Australia again—or anywhere else his reach extends. Dad needs specialized care for the rest of his life, and it won't be long before Mum can't cope on her own anymore, even with me helping where I can. If I can't support my parents financially, Raif, what am I to do?"

Fourteen

Raif held her close. He was still trying to assimilate the news that she hadn't gotten rid of their baby, along with the information she'd just given him. She was trembling now—with emotion, with fear and with helplessness. He understood it all. Had gone through it all himself when Burton had flung his cruel gibes in Raif's direction. But there was one thing Burton hadn't counted on: that Raif would do anything for his family, no matter what. Family always came first—including his unborn child and that baby's mother.

He eased her away slightly and tilted her face up to his. "Shanal, answer one thing. Do you trust me?"

Her lips quivered and she drew in a sharp breath. Her irises were all but consumed by the pupils of her eyes as she stared up into his face. "Yes, I do. I trust you."

"Then believe me when I say I will help you, if you'll just let me. Get me a copy of the loan agreement your father had with the bank. I'll ensure that the debt he owes Burton disappears. And trust me when I say that I can more than adequately provide for your parents, Shanal. And for you and our baby, too."

"But what about my work?" she protested. "Burton doesn't make idle threats. He'll spread out his tentacles and make it impossible for me to work anywhere."

Anyone else might have thought her concern about her work a selfish one, but Raif *knew* Shanal. She was, at heart, a geek. A lovable, intense, scarily clever geek. Her work meant so much to her, and she took justifiable pride in her professional accomplishments. Without her job she would feel as though she had no definition in life. It was as much a part of her as those perfectly arched eyebrows or the delectable texture and taste of her skin. And she had a fair share of her father's pride, as well. He knew, without question, that if Burton destroyed her reputation—which he was more than capable of doing—he might as well just grind her into the ground along with it.

It was up to Raif to make sure that didn't happen.

"I don't want you to worry about that. It's not going to be your problem. Just leave it with me."

"Raif, that's a lot of trust you're asking me to give. It's already Wednesday. We get married on Saturday afternoon."

"No, it won't get that far."

"But how on earth can you prevent it?"

"I just need you to trust me, Shanal. Can you continue to act as if you're going along with his plans?"

"Of course I can. I've managed to get this far."

He pressed a kiss to her lips. "That's my girl," he said approvingly. "I will fix this. I promise. Your parents will be okay and your job will be safe."

"But how—?"

"Trust me. Everything will be okay."

A knock at the door prevented Shanal from asking any more questions. As they acknowledged Ethan's presence and his summons to join the rest of the guests at the table for dinner, Raif quietly vowed that there was no way he would ever allow Burton to have any more power over Shanal or her family. Or anyone else, if he had any say in the matter.

By Thursday afternoon Raif was climbing the walls with frustration. The private-investigation company he'd retained to look into Burton's affairs had come highly recommended, but given the tiny window of time they had to work in, would they be able to dig up enough dirt on Rogers soon enough to make a difference?

Shanal had emailed a scanned copy of her parents' original loan agreement. The sum was staggering, but not impossible to meet out of his private resources. Raif was already in talks with his bank and financial planners to liquidate the necessary funds to ensure that sum Rogers had paid through a company facade, together with the appropriate market rate of interest, would be available to be settled, and the mortgage, also registered in that company's name, discharged. But the information he needed to nail Burton's ass to the wall, and ensure it stayed there—information necessary to keep Shanal from losing her job and her professional reputation—still eluded him.

He thought back through what he knew of the man. Always competitive at school, Burton had never excelled purely for the pleasure of it—no, he'd excelled because he felt he *had* to be the best, the fastest, the brightest. If another student's marks beat his in one exam, it hadn't been long before that student began to slide back in his work, or—even more sinisterly—was found with a copy of an exam paper, or alcohol, or even worse things, in his locker.

It wasn't that Rogers wasn't a clever man—he most definitely was, which made him all the more powerful an adversary. But there was a clinical air about him. As if he was detached from the world he lived in, choosing to lord it above everyone, and carefully selecting the things and people he wanted in his realm. And he'd chosen Shanal.

It was easy to see why. Intelligent, good at her work and incredibly beautiful into the bargain, she would have appeared to him like a prized exotic flower to be collected by an avid botanist. Raif had no doubt that Burton had bided his time before approaching Shanal. That was part of his modus operandi. He liked to stalk for a while, to savor his victory before pouncing.

It was how Burton had seduced Laurel away from Raif, striking when she was at a low moment. A month before the canyoneering trip, they'd argued, after Raif had once again avoided discussing the future of their relationship. The weekend they'd broken up, he'd used that dreadful adage, the one that usually struck fear into the heart of any person in a long-term relationship— he had told her that he "just needed a bit of space." So she'd given it to him.

Raif had loved Laurel, but not in the way he now knew he loved Shanal—and maybe, deep down, she'd sensed that, too. Maybe she'd known, on some level, that his dedication to her hadn't been as deep as hers for him. He'd certainly enjoyed their relationship, had even believed they were on the same page when it came to their time together—and, yes, maybe in time his feelings would have deepened and they would have married. But it hadn't happened fast enough for Laurel, and she had begun to ask for more from their relationship. Things including a commitment he hadn't been prepared, at that stage, to give to her or to anyone.

Either way, Raif still blamed himself for her death that awful day. He should have known she'd continue with the expedition without him. And if he'd been there for her as he should have been, Raif knew she wouldn't have died. He might have a reputation as a bit of a daredevil, but he never underestimated danger and always double-checked—no, *triple*-checked—everything when it came to equipment and environment in the pursuit of adventure sports.

Remembering Laurel made Raif wonder again if there should have been more to the reports that had been submitted to the coroner after her death. Was it possible that some vital information had been withheld? There were only two survivors from that day. One was Burton, the other was the guide. Raif picked up his phone and punched in the number for the investigator who had been assigned to him. After a brief conversation, directing the man to explore deeper into the circumstances of Laurel's death, and to talk directly with the guide who'd been with them that day, he hung up his phone.

Could the guide be the key? The man had sworn he'd checked the ropes and carabiner that had connected them. He had no reason to lie about that, or did he?

It was Friday evening when Raif got a call from the private investigator. He'd tracked down the guide, who'd said he would speak only to Raif. The investigator gave him the details of where to meet the man.

Raif fired a quick text message off to Shanal: Trust me!

It took him a while to find the address the investigator had given him, but Raif was persistent, eventually spotting the overgrown driveway on the hill road. He parked his car and walked toward the house. The front door opened as he approached. He recognized the guide immediately; Raif and Laurel had used him several times before her fatal expedition.

"Noah, good to see you," Raif said, stepping forward and offering his hand.

"Good to see you, too," the other man replied.

But he didn't meet his eyes as they shook hands ,and Raif had to admit to some shock at Noah's appearance. Was he sick? Always lean, the guy was almost skeletal in appearance now. And even though Noah was a good five years younger than Raif, right now he looked at least ten or fifteen years older.

Raif followed him inside and sat down in the living room. There was a layer of dust on every surface, and although the room held quality furnishings, an air of neglect hung over everything.

"Can I get you anything?" Noah offered, looking out from a face that was more gray than tan.

"No, I'm good, mate. You know why I'm here. Let's cut to the chase, huh? I don't have a lot of time."

Noah huffed a breath. "Yeah, time. I seem to have all too much of it."

"You're not guiding anymore?"

"I did a few trips after that day, but to be honest, since then…" His voice petered out and he shook his head.

Noah reached for a packet of cigarettes on the table. His hand shook as he tapped one out and raised it to his lips to light it. He drew deeply on the cigarette, taking his time to blow out the smoke before talking again. It was a habit Raif had never seen the man indulge in before. He'd always thought Noah was like him, testing himself against nature and the elements. Taking his highs from the thrill of living, not through stimulants like tobacco.

"He paid me."

Raif sat up a little straighter. "Burton?"

"Yeah." Noah took another long drag on his cigarette. "I'm so sorry, mate… I accepted the money. I said I wouldn't tell what really happened that day. He was so forceful. I could see her—lying there, at the bottom of the water hole, and he was arguing with me, physically holding me back from getting down to her. He told me he'd send me over the edge, too. He was actually holding me right there on the lip, with my back to the falls, telling me how much money he'd pay me if I just kept my mouth shut. In the end I said yes so he'd let me go…so I could attempt to retrieve Laurel…but I was too late. Once I realized she was gone, I guess I figured it didn't matter what I said, one way or another. The truth wasn't going to bring her back."

Conflicting emotions swelled and ebbed inside Raif. Noah had lied to save his own life, that much was clear. As much as it went against Raif's sense of honor, he could accept that, under the circumstances, Noah had felt as though he had no other choice.

"You said Burton held you back from checking on her. Did you think she might have still been alive at that point?"

"I couldn't be certain. She hit her head pretty hard on the way down, but there was still a chance. If I could have just gotten her out of the pool, I could have at least tried to save her. We were all trained for that kind of rescue. You know the saying. Train for the worst, expect the best. I lived by that, mate. And he wouldn't even let me try."

Raif considered Noah's words. "Tell me how she fell. You checked the equipment, right?"

Noah nodded. "I did. In fact she had been laughing at me, teasing me a bit for being so cautious—you know what she was like. Kind of flirty and fun, even when she was about to drop off a cliff face. I guess Burton didn't like that too much. He took her aside before she went over. I couldn't hear exactly what he was saying, but he didn't sound pleased. I did hear her reply, though. She told him to stop acting like a jealous child and to lighten up. I could see that made him mad.

"She'd already set her own anchors, Raif, three of them. He said he'd check them and her rope, and then she went over."

"It was the rope that came undone, wasn't it?"

"The knot slipped, yeah."

"Did you see him touch it?" A sick feeling gripped Raif's gut. "Or loosen it?"

Noah stubbed out his cigarette, lit another. "Yeah. I didn't realize it at the time or I'd have done something. You have to believe me on that."

Raif barely heard him, though. He couldn't quite come to terms with the shocking truth. Burton had knowingly tampered with Laurel's equipment. His actions had directly led to her death—a death he had further ensured by making certain Noah was unable to rescue or revive her. The ramifications were huge.

Raif rubbed his eyes and leaned back in the chair. He'd always known Burton was driven, dangerous even, but this was an entirely new level, even for him.

"He told me he'd just wanted to teach her a lesson.

Give her a fright, you know. He didn't expect the knot to fail completely."

Raif had to swallow down his anger and frustration. A beautiful life lost, and for what? One man's ego? It was beyond comprehension.

"Are you willing to swear to this, Noah?"

The younger man nodded. "Look at me, man. I can't live with myself any longer. Yes, he gave me money and I spent it, but since that day I haven't slept a full night or been able to work. Every time I tried to guide a group I'd have a panic attack and relive that day all over again. I'm done with that. I lied to the police and I'll take the rap for what I did, but he has to be held to justice, too. For Laurel's sake."

"Oh, he will be, I promise you that. And I'll get you help, Noah."

"Nah, man, I'm done. I made my choices that day— they were wrong, but I made them. I need to take responsibility for that and then maybe I can learn to live with it, and myself."

Raif made a mental note to ensure that Noah received the psychological and legal help he'd need. Sure, he'd done wrong, but he needed support now that he was trying to do the right thing. "Noah, you were a victim, too."

"I may have been, but I didn't pay the ultimate price like Laurel did. You have to stop him, Raif. The guy's dangerous."

"I will, rest assured. Are you prepared to come with me to the police station to make a statement?"

Noah looked around him, then back at Raif. "Money's not all it's cracked up to be, is it? Not if you can't live with yourself."

Raif stood up and looked down at the shell of the man who'd once been a vibrant, fit and happy person.

"That's true, but you're doing the right thing, Noah. And I meant what I said about helping you."

Noah stood, too, and shook his head. "I don't deserve it, but thank you."

It was a simple matter to head to the nearest police station and for Noah to make his statement. Raif was mindful of how late it was getting, but this situation wasn't something that could be rushed.

By the time Noah was finished, he was exhausted, but Raif could see how a weight had lifted from the man's shoulders. Maybe there'd be hope for him yet, Raif thought, as they shook hands and parted ways.

Fifteen

"Are you sure you want to do this, *meri pyaari beti*?"

"It will be okay," Shanal replied, as her mother finished dressing her once again in the much-loathed bridal gown. Shanal frowned in distaste at the reflection in the full-length mirror in her parents' bedroom. The dress was a symbol of everything Burton was. Show and glamor with very little substance.

She felt sick with nerves, which was not much of a change from the nausea that usually assailed her upon waking each morning. What would she do if Raif didn't show up in time to call a halt to the wedding? He'd asked her to trust him, and she did, but that didn't stop fear from creeping up from the shadows in her mind.

Burton had exposed a side of himself that she'd never thought possible. If anyone had told her back when they first got engaged that he could be cruel and manipulative like that she would not have believed it. Now, of course, was a different story. She couldn't believe she'd been so oblivious to his true nature. Granted, she'd never been all that attracted to him—certainly not in the way that Raif set her blood pumping and her heart skittering.

To think she'd even initially felt guilty about using Burton to solve her problems. It was enough to make her doubt her own judgment. If she'd made a mistake like that, was she making an even worse one by trusting Raif to make her problems go away? Surely she should be capable of doing that herself?

She looked up in the mirror and studied her reflection again, and that of her mother as she fussed and tweaked with the fall of the new veil until it was just so. Shanal reminded herself she was a capable woman. She'd gained a doctorate in her field. She'd written respected papers. She ran the lab at Burton International without fault or flaw. She wasn't weak or incapable— she was just in over her head. And in those circumstances, it showed how intelligent she was that she was willing to let someone else lend a hand. Despite all the things she could do on her own, she needed help now.

Her mother's eyes met hers in the mirror, a question behind them. *What if Raif doesn't show?*

"It will be all right, you'll see," Shanal said, injecting as much enthusiasm into her voice as she could. "Everything will be all right."

Her parents had chosen not to come to the church this time. Her mother had argued that it had been hard enough last time to get her father out of the house and to the cathedral, where he'd felt the eyes of everyone around them as he'd accompanied Shanal in his wheelchair. Shanal had agreed. Besides, it wasn't as if this wedding was going to go ahead. At least she fervently hoped not. Her hand strayed to her belly, where Raif's child nestled safe and secure inside her.

She had to do this. She had to go through the motions for her child and for Raif. He'd promised he'd find a solution to her problems and she had to believe he would. He was, she thought with a private smile, a Masters, after all. They were not the type of people to ever quit. Knowing that gave her the inner strength she needed, and she straightened her posture and squared her shoulders.

The car Burton had arranged to collect her and to take her to the church would be here any minute now. After one final check in the mirror, she turned away. Her father was in his chair in the sitting room, staring out the window. She bent before him and took his limp hands in hers. Hands that had supported her as a baby and held hers as she'd balanced on walls and jumped waves at the beach. Hands that had saved so many lives over so many years. Hands that had taken one.

"It will be all right, Dad. I don't want you to worry anymore. It's all going to work itself out." She leaned forward and kissed him, gently squeezing his hands in reassurance before repeating, "Like I just told Mum, everything is going to be okay."

The words continued to echo like a mantra, over and over in her mind, as the car took her to the cathedral from where, only seven weeks ago, she'd fled. From where Raif had rescued her. Would he get here in time to do it again? She had to believe he would. She just had to, because the alternative was not worth considering.

As the driver opened her door and offered her a hand to help her alight, she caught a glimpse of the crystal encrusted satin pumps she wore. Perhaps running shoes would have been a better choice, she thought cynically.

But then, she had no more need to run. Not with Raif at her back.

She ascended the stairs to the cathedral and was greeted by the priest, who took a few minutes with her.

"Is everything okay today, my dear?" he asked, concern drawing his bushy white brows together. "You're certain about this?"

She nodded, unable to enunciate the words that he sought from her. It would be a lie if she said she was sure. She had never been more uncertain about anything. With every second that ticked past she came that much closer to having to go through with marrying Burton.

"Shall we start?" she asked, with as much of a smile as she could muster.

"Certainly. I'll bring Burton out to you."

"B-Burton?"

"Yes, he said that given what happened last time, he wanted to escort you in himself. No need for nerves this time around."

The priest opened the door and made a small gesture with his hand. Shanal was forced to swallow against the bitter taste in her mouth as Burton joined her. As soon as they were alone his eyes swept her from head to toe.

"You look beautiful," he said, as if that was all that mattered. And to him, it probably was. "Are you ready?"

She inclined her head and Burton took her hand and placed it on his forearm.

"Good, we look perfect together. I so look forward to dancing with you at our reception."

With any luck there would be no reception, she thought fervently. Music began inside the church and she and Burton started to walk down the aisle. She was surprised at the number of people there. She'd asked for this wedding to be simpler and smaller, but she'd left those details to Burton to arrange, and clearly he'd chosen to ignore her preferences. Anyway, she supposed that none of it mattered anymore. Burton had never taken her wishes into account before, so it shouldn't surprise her that he wouldn't have over this. The sight of so many friends and colleagues made her all the more uncomfortable in the overdone confection of fabric and diamantes that he'd insisted she wear again. But, she made a mental reminder, she would stand here today as *herself*, not as Burton Roger's puppet bride. At least she wouldn't be if Raif got here in time. Where was he?

She scanned the many faces turned to them as they walked down the aisle, searching for Raif's dark head, his square shoulders. He was nowhere to be seen. Fear tightened its screws on her already tightly strung nerves. He wasn't going to make it!

At the altar the priest gave a brief welcome before launching into the service.

"We are gathered here today…" he began, with a wink at the bride and groom before him.

Struck by a near overwhelming sense of déjà vu, Shanal flung a frightened look toward the door. Still no sign of Raif. Firm, almost painful pressure on her hands made her look up into Burton's eyes, where the hard gleam of satisfaction reflected back at her. He was getting what he wanted and she could do nothing to stop it. The feeling of powerlessness was terrifying, but nowhere near as frightening as the cruel smile that curved Burton's lips.

How had she ever thought that marrying him would be a good idea? How had she allowed him to gain so much control over her? She knew all too well that the fault lay with her. She'd gone into this with two objectives: her parents' financial security and the head research position at Burton International. She hadn't ever believed she could lose her soul in exchange for those things. She should have known better than to try and strike a deal with the devil.

"If anyone here has just cause why Burton and Shanal may not be lawfully joined together, let them speak now or forever hold their peace."

Burton fired a seething glare at the priest. "I thought I told you to take that out of the service."

"It's a requirement, dear boy, but don't worry. Everything will be all ri—"

His words were cut off as the front doors to the cathedral clanged open and a loud male voice rang out.

"Stop the wedding. I object!"

Shanal sagged in relief as she saw Raif stride toward the altar, a look of grim determination on his face.

"Oh, not again," the priest groaned, his face paling.

"Keep going," Burton insisted, his own face suffusing with ugly, angry color.

"We can't," the cleric whispered back. "He has to state his objection."

"There's nothing he can say that can stop this wedding, trust me."

"Let's find out, shall we?"

The priest looked at Raif. Everyone looked at him, including Shanal, who had never seen a more welcome sight in all her life. Her eyes raked over him, taking in his disheveled hair and the determined light burning in those beautiful blue eyes of his. He stood there, tall and proud, dressed in a casual windbreaker and worn jeans and boots, and to her, he'd never looked more appealing.

"Young man, please state your objection," the priest directed.

"Before I do, I need to know one thing."

"What is that?"

Raif looked directly at Shanal, his expression intense and sure. "Shanal, do you love me?"

There was a collective gasp around the cathedral.

"Don't answer him!" Burton interrupted, stepping forward, his hands clenched.

Shanal moved swiftly to insert herself between the two men. The air between them seethed with testosterone. She turned her back to Burton and faced Raif, her eyes meeting his. Love him? She hadn't wanted to think about that through all of this, but now, with him here before her, she knew the truth without doubt.

She breathed for him. Her heart beat for him. Her body yearned for him.

"I do. I love you, Raif Masters, with all my heart and with everything I am."

Raif's lips quirked in a half smile that made her want to stretch up and kiss him with all the devotion and passion that dwelled inside her.

"That's perfect, then. Because you know I love you, too."

Two policemen appeared in the doorway to the cathedral, drawing everyone's attention.

"Good, thank goodness. Finally someone with some sense," Burton blustered. "Please, come and arrest this man. He's disrupting my wedding and being a public nuisance."

"I don't think so, Burt," Raif replied, his smile widening as he did so.

Shanal saw Burton bristle at the loathed shortening of his name.

"This is preposterous. Get this man out of here," he directed the two officers, who'd drawn level with Raif.

"No, Burton, they're not here for me. They're here for you, and this time you're not getting off without the blame that's been due to you for far too long."

"Don't be ridiculous. I don't know what you're talking about."

Burton stood even more upright, as if by doing so he could convince everyone what a model citizen he was. But Shanal knew better. She knew the darkness that lurked beneath the surface of his smooth facade. She understood the latent danger he kept well hidden under that apparently charming and debonair exterior.

Raif caught the priest's attention. "Father, I object to this marriage on the grounds that this man is a criminal. His deliberate, spiteful actions led to the death of an innocent woman three years ago, after which he deliberately withheld the truth from a police investigation and perverted the course of justice by bribing others to hide the truth."

Burton paled, his eyes narrowing at Raif as he directed the full force of his hatred toward him. "You're lying. It's all lies," he said, his voice cold and deadly as finely honed steel. "You will regret this, Masters."

"I don't think so," Raif replied just as smoothly. "You won't get away with it this time. The police have a full statement from Noah. It seems he couldn't live with hiding the truth."

The officers stepped forward, one on either side of Burton. "Sir, you need to come with us."

Burton launched himself toward Raif, a feral expression on his face. "You think you've won? You haven't—you can't win. *I'm* the winner. I remember how you mooned about her when we were at school. How lovelorn you were when you thought no one was looking. When she came to work for me I knew there was nothing that would stop me from getting her. I had had Laurel, now I have Shanal. She's mine, I tell you!"

The police grabbed Burton's arms and pulled him back before he could do more than unleash his diatribe.

"Take him away." Raif nodded to the officers, but Burton, it seemed, hadn't said quite enough.

"I waited a long time to lord it over you the way you did over me at school. You think it didn't hurt when we were growing up, when you excelled at everything— the way you thought you were so superior because you always won at sports, with your grades or with girls? I vowed a long time ago I would beat you, and I did. Shanal is mine."

The look in Burton's eyes held a hint of mania that sent a thread of fear winding through Raif's heart. The man was dangerous, and far less stable than Raif had realized. Had he truly done all this—manipulated everyone so cruelly—because of some petty school yard grudge?

"She's her own person," Raif said quietly. "She makes her own choices."

One of the policemen recited the charges against Burton and then read him his rights before they escorted him, still struggling, from the cathedral. Raif and Shanal watched in silence. Around them, the silence changed to a loud hum of excited murmurs.

Raif looked at Shanal and offered her his hand. "Shall we go?"

"Please."

His strong fingers closed around hers and together they walked outside. Raif's Maserati was parked at the curb and he held the door open for her, then made sure her dress was completely tucked inside before closing the door. Shanal sat in the comfortable leather seat and let relief wash over her in drenching waves. Burton's hold on her was over.

Raif settled in the seat beside her. His face was more serious than she'd ever seen it.

"You're safe now," he said firmly. "Safe from him, safe to do what you choose. He can't control you anymore."

"What will happen now?"

"He'll be formally charged and questioned. Given it's the weekend, it might be a while before he comes up before the court. I don't imagine he'll be happy about cooling his heels in jail so his lawyer will try and have him released on bail. The police assure me that, due to his easy access to unlimited funds, they consider him a flight risk and will do everything in their power to ensure he remains behind bars."

Shanal sighed in relief, then looked deep into Raif's eyes. "And us? What will happen with us?"

"That's entirely up to you. Would you like me to take you to your parents' place?"

She shook her head. "No, I'd like to call them, let them know I'm all right—that this business with Burton is over—but I want to be with you. I want to be wherever you are."

His eyes darkened at her words and he leaned forward, pressing his lips all too briefly against hers. "If that's what the lady wants, then that's what the lady will get."

He started the car and drove away from the cathedral. Shanal briefly looked back at the people now spilling from the church doors and down the steps. She shuddered at the thought of how different it all could have been if Raif hadn't made it on time, if he hadn't discovered the information that had put a stop to Burton's manipulation. She turned her head to look forward again, to her future. A future that, hopefully, would include the man next to her, for a long time to come.

When they pulled in through the gates that led to Raif's home, Shanal knew she was in the right place. He stopped at the front door and came around to help her from the low-slung car. When he led her inside she couldn't help feeling how different this was than the last time she'd been here. Then, she'd been filled with anxiety. Now, nothing could be further from her mind.

Raif gestured to his office. "Use the phone in there to call your mum and dad. I'll go pour us a drink."

She smiled in thanks and went into the room. Her mother answered on the first ring.

"Mum, it's okay. It's all over. The police have Burton now."

"What—? The police?"

"I'll explain it all to you and Dad later. I promise."

"What about the mortgage and the loan?"

"Raif said he'd take care of everything. I believe him, Mum. You can, too." And she meant every word. After what Raif had done today she would trust him with her life.

"Oh, thank God for that. When are you coming home?"

"Soon. I'm with Raif now. He's where I belong." As she said the words, she knew she'd never belong anywhere else—with anyone else—more than she did with him.

"Then that is good. Have you talked yet? About the baby?"

"Not properly. But Mum, don't worry, and tell Dad everything will be all right now."

By the time she hung up, Shanal felt drained. Even

so, the weight of responsibility that had so burdened her these past months had lifted. Yes, there was a great deal to sort out and work through, but she could see an end in sight. A happier end. One that began with the man waiting for her across the hall.

Raif was struck anew by Shanal's beauty and grace as she walked toward him, the overblown fussiness of her gown serving to accentuate the classical beauty of the darkness of her hair and the burnished bronze of her skin. He handed her the glass of mineral water he'd poured for her, and lifted his wine in a toast.

"To us," he said.

"Yes, to us."

Shanal clinked her glass against his and took a sip.

"You okay?" Raif studied her, sensing that she was in a state of turmoil.

"Just thinking, wondering what's going to happen next with Burton International, with my parents' home, with you and me."

"Let me put your mind at rest about the first two," Raif said, leading her over to the sofa and sitting down next to her. He stretched one arm along the back of the couch and brushed her cheek with his fingertips. "The board will step in at Burton International and keep things running. He'll be removed as CEO and a provisional one will be installed in his place."

"How do you know all this?" she asked.

He smiled in return. It hadn't been easy and it had taken the better part of the morning to meet with the movers and shakers who would take control of the company. But they hadn't needed much convincing when he'd explained that Burton would be arrested on a manslaughter charge, at the very least, before the wedding.

More importantly, he'd done it in time to save Shanal from committing herself to a man who treated people as if they were no more than accessories designed to make him look all the more powerful or appealing.

"I know some people," he said, keeping the details to a minimum. There'd be time enough to go into the specifics of how things would pan out.

"And my parents? The mortgage Burton held over their house?"

"All sorted out. He didn't hold that personally. It was done through a company run by some of the same people on the Burton International board. The mortgage will be discharged in full on Monday, as soon as business opens."

Tears brightened the pale green of Shanal's eyes. Raif took her glass from her and put it with his on the table in front of them. He then turned to pull her into his arms.

"I can't believe it's over," she whispered against his chest.

"It's only just begun," he murmured in response.

He put a finger under her chin and lifted her face to his, capturing her lips in a kiss that conveyed all the promise and hope he had for the future, their future. She was quick to respond. Her hands reached up to cup his face, to hold him to her as if she would never let him go. And he didn't want her to. He'd waited a long time for this woman. He planned to hold on to her for the rest of their lives.

She protested when he broke their kiss, but came willingly when he stood and took her hands. He led her down the hall toward his master suite, to the place where he could show her, by words and by deed, exactly what she meant to him.

"Raif?"

"Hmm?"

"I meant what I said in the cathedral. I do love you. Not just because you rescued me, again. Not just because you promised to make everything right for me and my parents. But because you make me happier than I've ever been. And what makes me happiest of all is the thought of a future with you and our child."

An incredible swell of joy filled him. She'd put into words the most astounding gift of all.

"Thank you. You humble me," he replied, resting his forehead against hers and hooking his arms around her waist. "I would move heaven and earth for you and our child. I want you to know that. All you ever need to do is ask."

"Just love me back. That's all I'll ever want or need."

"I do. Let me show you exactly how much."

He took his time undressing her, in undoing the row of crystal buttons down her back until her exquisite beauty was revealed without adornment. As he did so, he traced the lines of her body with his fingers, with his tongue, with his lips. She trembled beneath his touch— not with fear or discomfort, but with need and want that was a mirror to his own. And when he lifted her into his arms and laid her gently on his bed, he knew he could explore her every day and never tire of her.

Shanal watched him from under hooded lids as he stripped away his own clothing with far less finesse than he'd undressed her. His erection jutted from his body, his flesh aching to find surcease within her. When he joined her on the bed her hands were quick to find him, to stroke his length, to cup his balls, to squeeze gently, making him close his eyes and give himself over to trust. Trust in her the way she'd trusted him.

They kissed, their lips fusing. First soft and gentle,

then with increasing heat until Raif felt as though his entire body was aflame with want for her. His tongue probed the moist recess of her mouth, stroking her tongue as it met his, teasing the roof of her mouth in a kiss that was hot and wet and deep. Shanal arched her back, pressing her breasts against his chest. He tore his mouth from hers, then kissed a trail across her jawline, down her throat and farther, until he caught one nipple between his lips.

His teeth grazed the taut bud and he felt her shake beneath him, her fingers digging into his back, her nails tiny points of pleasure-pain as he drew the hardened tip deeper into his mouth and pulled with his teeth and his tongue.

"I love you, Shanal, and I'm going to show you just how much," he growled against her skin, pressing kisses lower and lower down her body.

She moaned in delight as his hands spread her thighs, as he nuzzled her neatly trimmed thatch of dark hair. Her hips bowed upward as he licked the curve of her groin. His mouth found her center, his tongue flicking against the bead of nerve endings he knew would tip her completely over the edge. Again and again he stroked that tiny pearl. Beneath his hands he felt the muscles in her legs grow tense, then begin to tremble as a wave rode through her body, then another and another until she collapsed against the bed, gasping.

Her fingers tangled lazily in his hair, traced tiny circles against his scalp. Raif rose over her again, fitting his body against hers. When he looked down at her face he felt a deep sense of pride that he'd finally chased away her shadows—that this beautiful creature was his as much as he was hers, and that he'd made her as happy as she deserved to be.

He fitted himself between her legs, nudging his arousal against her hot, wet center. He groaned as his tip slid into her body.

"Yes," she whispered to him, her hands at his hips, pulling him, urging him to go all the way. "Be mine."

"Always," he answered, kissing her and allowing his length to slide deep inside her.

She was heat and velvet, all in one. Her inner muscles tightened around him, drawing him deeper. The act of joining with another human being had never felt so perfect or so right. He pulled back and then slid home again, slow and sure—taking every second, every sensation, and savoring it as the extraordinary gift it was.

"I love you, Raif," Shanal cried, holding him tight.

This was the ultimate in life, he thought fleetingly. This was perfection. And then he let instinct take over, and the moment became a blur of unique pleasure, of giving and receiving, and finally, of completion as they climaxed together in a kaleidoscope of sensual gratification.

When his heart rate had returned to something approximating normal, Raif rolled to his side, holding Shanal in his arms as if she was the most precious thing in his world. She was and, God willing, always would be. Only one thing more would make this moment perfect.

He pulled away slightly so he could see her face, then drew in a long breath.

"Shanal, I want you to know that I will always be here for you and—" he pressed his hand across her lower belly "—our baby. I know you are most probably sick of weddings by now, but when you're ready, would you do me the utmost honor of becoming my wife?"

Her perfectly formed lips pulled into a smile. "I think

I can find it in me to walk down the aisle once more, as long as you're the one waiting for me at the other end. But it will definitely be the last time," she teased, tracing the line of his nose with a fingertip. Then her expression grew serious and she nodded. "I would love to be your wife, Raif. It would be my greatest privilege to spend the rest of my life with you and to raise our children together."

"I'm glad to hear it," he answered with a smile. "Because if you'd said no, I might have had to whisk you away on a houseboat once again, and this time never let you go."

She shook her head. "You don't ever need to worry about that. I'm yours, for always. As you are mine."

Epilogue

Raif turned to watch his family as they took their seats in the marquee on the lawn at The Masters, his infant son, dressed in a baby tuxedo, cradled in his arms. In the background, the vineyard stretched out over the hillside, and farther in the distance, the dark silhouette of the old family mansion stood sentinel on top of the hill. The setting had a permanence and sense of history that he'd always enjoyed. It was good to know that some things never changed. But as he looked around at everyone gathered here at the family home to celebrate the birth of his and Shanal's first child, and their wedding, it was also good to see the future shaping and changing with each new member of the family.

"Here, you better give me that baby," his mother said, bustling over to his side. "You're spoiling him rotten, you know. He needs his grandmother's firm hand."

Raif relinquished his son with a laugh. "Mum, you

know you're the family softie. Besides, haven't you always said you can never spoil a baby?"

"Very true. But I have a feeling your hands are going to be all too full very shortly. Don't you have a wedding to enjoy?"

"I do," he said with a wide smile. "And I'm looking forward to it."

"Well, you've both waited long enough. It's a shame Shanal's dad didn't live long enough to see her happily married."

"Yeah, but at least he found peace before he went. He saw her happy, and that's the main thing, right? And he knew we'd be naming our little guy Curtis, after him."

Marianne Masters patted her eldest son lovingly on one cheek. "You're a good man, Raif Masters. I'm so proud of you."

"I love you, Mum."

Ethan arrived beside him, dressed in a dinner suit and with a boutonniere affixed to his lapel. He raised the one he held in his hand. "Your turn," he said, pinning the flower to his cousin's suit jacket. "And we need to go line up. Apparently, your bride is ready."

"Then what are we waiting for?" Raif asked.

Together they walked toward the temporary altar that had been set up beneath the decorated marquee on the grounds. The June weather had been kind so far and the predicted rain had held off.

"What's the latest on Burton Rogers?" Ethan asked. "The case against him still hasn't gone to court yet, has it?"

"I'm told his lawyers are dragging it out—fighting to have him declared mentally unfit to stand trial. Either way, he'll be put away for a long time and he won't be able to hurt the people I love ever again."

"They should lock people like him up forever," Ethan said emphatically.

"I couldn't agree more."

Raif and Ethan joined Raif's brother, Cade, and the celebrant who stood waiting. Raif turned to face the aisle that Shanal would be coming down. As he listened for the music that would cue her arrival, he studied the faces before him. His parents sat in front, looking exceptionally proud and happy. Their trip to France had whetted their appetite for more travel and they had a trip to Tuscany planned for the European autumn. Whether his father succeeded in taking Marianne away from baby Curtis for more than a month would be the test, though, Raif thought.

His cousins Judd Wilson and Nicole Jackson were also there with their respective spouses, Anna and Nate. Anna bore a delicate bump, announcing her early pregnancy. Ethan's sister, Tamsyn, sat a row back with her husband, Finn Gallagher, who was propping their sleeping five-month-old daughter on one shoulder. Beside Tamsyn was her half sister, Alexis, who together with her husband, Raoul, was busy reining in their twin boys. The toddlers were charming and delightful, but also well-skilled at keeping their parents on their toes. The boys' half sister, Ruby, a month shy of her third birthday, was to be Shanal's flower girl, and Raif had heard that she'd been delighted when she was shown the miniature sari she would wear today.

And then the sound of delicate notes wrought from violin strings dragged his attention back to the house, to where his bride now appeared on the back veranda, together with her mother and Ruby. She was a resplendent vision in red and gold, eschewing a white bridal gown for her mother's traditions, and to Raif she'd never looked more beautiful. His eyes never left her as, with her mother by her side, she followed Ruby down the aisle. Shanal grinned at him in return. They turned together to face the celebrant, who smiled at them both, then began.

"We are gathered here today…"

"No running away this time," Raif whispered to his bride as the celebrant intoned in the background.

"Never again," Shanal answered. "I have everything I want right here, with you."

* * * * *

If you loved this story from
USA TODAY *bestselling author*
Yvonne Lindsay, pick up the books in
THE MASTER VINTNERS *series:*

THE WAYWARD SON
A FORBIDDEN AFFAIR
ONE SECRET NIGHT
THE HIGH PRICE OF SECRETS
WANTING WHAT SHE CAN'T HAVE

All available now from Harlequin Desire!

If you're on Twitter, tell us
what you think of Harlequin Desire!
#harlequindesire

COMING NEXT MONTH FROM

HARLEQUIN
Desire

Available April 7, 2015

#2365 FOR HIS BROTHER'S WIFE
Texas Cattleman's Club: After the Storm
by Kathie DeNosky

Cole Richardson always resented how his first sweetheart married his twin brother. But now Paige Richardson is a widow, and the construction mogul sees his second chance. Maybe, just maybe, Paige is with the right Richardson this time...

#2366 THE NANNY PLAN
Billionaires and Babies • by Sarah M. Anderson

When Nate Longmire unexpectedly takes custody of his baby niece, the tech billionaire hires a temporary nanny. But what happens when Nate wants to make her position in the family—and in his heart—much more permanent?

#2367 TWINS ON THE WAY
The Kavanaghs of Silver Glen • by Janice Maynard

A wild night could have serious repercussions for Gavin Kavanagh. But even when he suspects he's been set up, he can't keep away from the sexy seducer...*especially* now that she's carrying his twins.

#2368 THE COWGIRL'S LITTLE SECRET
Red Dirt Royalty • by Silver James

Oil tycoon Cord Barron thought he'd never see Jolie Davis again. But she's back—with his little boy in tow. Now a custody battle is brewing, but what Cord really wants is to take passionate possession of this wayward cowgirl!

#2369 FROM EX TO ETERNITY
Newlywed Games • by Kat Cantrell

Wedding-dress designer Cara Chandler-Harris is forced to team up with her runaway groom for work at an island resort, and things quickly get personal. Will Mr. Boomerang turn into Mr. Forever this time around?

#2370 FROM FAKE TO FOREVER
Newlywed Games • by Kat Cantrell

Who are Meredith Chandler-Harris and fashion heir Jason Lynhurst kidding? What happens in Vegas never stays there! Now this "accidentally married" couple wonders if an impetuous fling can turn into happily-ever-after.

HDCNM0315

REQUEST YOUR FREE BOOKS!

2 FREE NOVELS PLUS 2 FREE GIFTS!

ALWAYS POWERFUL, PASSIONATE AND PROVOCATIVE

SPECIAL EXCERPT FROM

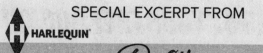
HARLEQUIN
Desire

*Disowned and pregnant after one passionate night in
Vegas, Cassidy Corelli shows up on the doorstep of the
only man who can help her...*

Read on for a sneak peek at
TWINS ON THE WAY,
the latest in USA TODAY *bestselling author*
Janice Maynard's
THE KAVANAGHS OF SILVER GLEN *series.*

Without warning, Gavin stood up. Suddenly the office
shrank in size. His personality and masculine presence
sucked up all the available oxygen. Pacing so near
Cassidy's chair that he almost brushed her knees, Gavin
shot her a look laden with frustration. "We need some
ground rules if you're going to stay with me while we sort
out this pregnancy, Cassidy. First of all, we're going to
forget that we've ever seen each other naked."

She gulped, fixating on the dusting of hair where the
shallow V-neck of his sweater revealed a peek of his
chest. "I'm pretty sure that's going to be the elephant in
the room. Our night in Vegas was amazing. Maybe not for
you, but for me. Telling me to forget it is next to impossible."

"Good Lord, woman. Don't you have any social
armor, at all?"

"I am not a liar. If you want me to pretend we haven't
been intimate, I'll try, but I make no promises."

He leaned over her, resting his hands on the arms of the chair. His beautifully sculpted lips were in kissing distance. Smoke-colored irises filled with turbulent emotions locked on hers like lasers. "I may be attracted to you, Cass, but I don't completely trust you. It's too soon. So, despite evidence to the contrary, I do have some self-control."

Maybe *he* did, but hers was melting like snow in the hot sun. His coffee-scented breath brushed her cheek. This close, she could see tiny crinkles at the corners of his eyes. She might have called them laugh lines if she could imagine her onetime lover being lighthearted enough and smiling long enough to create them.

"You're crowding my personal space," she said primly.

For several seconds, she was sure he was going to steal a kiss. Her breathing went shallow, her nipples tightened and a tumultuous feeling rose in her chest. Something volatile. For the first time, she understood that whatever madness had taken hold of them in Las Vegas was neither a fluke nor a solitary event.

Don't miss
TWINS ON THE WAY
by USA TODAY *bestselling author Janice Maynard.*

Available April 2015,
wherever Harlequin® Desire books and ebooks are sold.

www.Harlequin.com